D0960210

The House That Wasn't There

The House That Wasn't There

ELANA K. ARNOLD

WALDEN POND PRESS

An Imprint of HarperCollinsPublishers

The House That Wasn't There
Copyright © 2021 by Elana K. Arnold
All rights reserved. Printed in the United States of America.
No part of this book may be used or reproduced in any manner whatsoever
without written permission except in the case of brief quotations embodied
in critical articles and reviews. For information address HarperCollins
Children's Books, a division of HarperCollins Publishers, 195 Broadway,
New York, NY 10007.
www.harpercollinschildrens.com

Library of Congress Control Number: 2020947622
ISBN 978-0-06-293706-3

Typography by Molly Fehr
21 22 23 24 25 PC/LSCH   10 9 8 7 6 5 4 3 2 1

First Edition

For my family,
who helps me open every door

*O*nce, not very long ago, there were two houses side by side. In one house lived a boy; in the other lived no one. But that, and everything else, was about to change.

Let me tell you what happened.

CHAPTER 1

The boy's name was Alder. He was eleven and a half years old, and he had lived in the house at 15 Rollingwood Drive since before he could remember. In fact, he had been born there. In the bathtub, to be exact, something his mother liked to tell visitors to the home, something that Alder had been proud of until about two years ago when, suddenly, he was not.

Once, there had been three people who lived together at 15 Rollingwood Drive: Alder, his mother, Greta, and his father, whom everyone had called Canary because of his voice.

Alder had been just three years old when his father died, taken by a short, sudden illness. He had no memories of his father or his father's voice, except from the recordings he had left behind. Sometimes Alder wished that the recordings had been left for him alone, but the truth was that Canary's voice was quite well known, as he'd had a brief but brilliant flame of success, earning enough money before he died at thirty-one to ensure that Alder and his mother would never have to worry too much about money, as long as they were careful; as his mother liked to tell Alder, they had "a comfortable nest egg" upon which they could rely, as if that was all he needed to know.

Sometimes, though, when Alder was entirely alone, and when the room was very dark, and when he was no longer awake but also not yet quite asleep, he felt that he could remember something about his father—the smell of him, a sort of sharp burning like a just-smoked cigarette mixed with the fresh scent of new-cut grass.

Alder was not sure if that was a real memory. He could have asked his mother, for she was the kind of person who would tell him the truth whether he liked it or not. But he never shared this scent memory with her, partly because it was the only thing he had of his father that he didn't have to share with anyone else, and partly because it might not be a *real* memory at all, a possibility Alder did not know if he could bear.

The house at 15 Rollingwood Drive was small but neat. The floors were wood—scratched in some places; sun bleached in others, like under the wide front window and in patches where light shone through glass arches in the green door. The furniture, most of it, had been in the house as long as Alder could remember—the pink velvet couch in the front room that slumped a bit in the middle, where it had been sat upon the most; the wooden TV stand, with all the electrical gear atop it—the TV, of course, and the cable box, and Alder's gaming system, and various remote controls, which Alder's mom called "the clackers" even though they didn't clack.

In the afternoons, the front room was kept cool by the wide green foliage of the walnut tree outside. Though it technically sat in the neighbors' yard, it leaned toward his, as if it wanted to be closer. It cast its helpful shadow onto Alder's house, and that shadow was a comfortably reliable presence, growing and shrinking as daylight waxed and waned.

The fern that squatted and spread on the small round table next to the couch had lived there a long time too, but not as long as Alder and his mother; she had given him the fern four and a half years ago, for his seventh birthday, when Alder had gone through a short phase during which he considered a future career as a horticulturalist, after learning the term and thinking it sounded very important and interesting. After a few months, it had become clear that Alder was perhaps not horticulturally blessed, when his mother had to save the fern from a near death by thirst.

She'd moved it then from his bedroom to the front room, where she could "keep an eye on it," and Alder had felt vaguely relieved to have escaped the burden of having to keep the plant alive.

Aside from the couch and the electrical things and the fern, the house was filled with all the usual stuff—books and puzzles and stacks of papers. Old coffee tins full of pennies and buttons and nails. Baskets full of knitting stuff. And an opossum that wasn't alive anymore, but once had been, named Mort.

Mort had been an anniversary gift from Alder's dad to Alder's mom, before Alder had been born. Alder knew the story by heart: how his parents (before they were parents) had taken a trip to Seattle, where they toured the Space Needle and roamed Pike Place Market and stumbled upon Ballyhoo Curiosity Shop, a strange place in the basement of a building that boasted, among other things, a large set of insects preserved in clear resin, a variety of skulls and antique dolls, and an assortment of taxidermy, including a two-headed calf, a wall-mounted raccoon hind end, and Mort.

"I don't know why the opossum struck us as partic-ularly funny," Alder's mom had told him. "There were many other things, odder things, in the curiosity shop. But something about him—his teeth maybe, the way it almost looked as though he were smiling—sent both of us into an absolute hysteria. We were laughing so hard, we had to leave the shop. But a few months later, on our anniversary—our one-year wedding anniversary, to be exact—when I opened the box Canary put on my lap! It was that same opossum, smiling up at me." At this point in the story, Alder's mom always looked fondly at the opossum, who ruled over the front room from his position on the top shelf of the bookcase. "Your father had called the shop and paid for it by phone," she would say. "And here he is, even though Canary isn't." And then she'd stare a moment longer at the opossum, and then she'd blink, and she'd come back to the present moment, back to Alder. And she'd pat him on the knee or pull him into her side or kiss his forehead and stroke his hair.

Sometimes, when his mom wasn't around, like when she'd trust him to stay alone while she ran to the grocery store, or the odd occasions when he'd find himself awake early on a Sunday morning while his mother was still asleep, Alder would move a kitchen chair near to the book-case and climb up to take a closer look at the taxidermied opossum.

"Mort," Alder would whisper, and he'd click his finger-nail against a glass eye.

Of course, the opossum never answered.

Aside from that front room, there were the bedrooms—Alder's, his mother's, and a third, which was technically a bedroom even though it had no bed; the kitchen; the big bathroom (with the bathtub in which Alder had been born) and one small bathroom (with just a toilet and a sink); the eating nook attached to the kitchen; and the small rectangular dining room, where Alder did his homework and where he and his mother put together puzzles. The music stuff was in the dining room, because that was where they usually listened. The record player and records, and the newer stuff, too, the speakers that could play music streamed from a computer or cell phone.

It was at the dining room table, usually in the evenings, usually while puzzling, that Alder and his mother listened to his father's songs. In that room too hung the one portrait of the three of them, posed in front of the huge, beautiful walnut tree in the yard—Alder in the foreground upon his mother's lap, a fat round white baby with a shock of near-black curls and big, dark, blue eyes, framed by embarrassingly long lashes; his mother, hair longer then than now, dark blond with a touch of strawberry redness, parted in the middle and falling around Alder like a cape, a bright smile on her face, her eyes turned down toward the baby on her lap; and Canary standing behind them both, looking straight into the camera with a broad, happy grin, a hand on each of his wife's shoulders. His brown hair was brushed back from his brow. He wore a lustrous beard. He was—they all were—so very much *alive*.

It was folk music, Alder's mother told him, that Canary made. Alder sort of loved to listen to his father sing, and sort of hated it at the same time. His father had played the banjo, accompanying himself as he sang.

Wandering down the railroad tracks away from my sweet
    home
Wondering on the railroad tracks where I next will roam
Whispering on the railroad tracks why the wind has blown
Wandering down the railroad tracks away from my sweet
    home

Each note from the banjo was a wail, a twang, a whisper. And when Canary joined in, half the sounds out of his mouth weren't words at all, they were more like crooning and cooing and chirping. Maybe that was why they called him Canary; though his voice was deep and rich, not high and sharp, still, the rise and fall of it could tell a story, even without any words. And the banjo told its story too, as if to answer Canary's call. Slow, then fast, then slow again.

And Alder would sit, a puzzle piece in his hand, listening, as if maybe this time the song would have new words, better words. Words that *meant* something. But it never did.

In any case, other than the fact that his father was dead, Alder's life was rather unextraordinary; he lived in his

9

comfortable house, surrounded by the things he loved—the music and the bathtub, the pink couch and the puzzles, the clackers and Mort, with the walnut tree's gentle shadow and with his wonderful (though sometimes embarrassing) mother, at 15 Rollingwood Drive.

This was true, at least, until late summer, when the girl moved in next door, and Alder, for the first time in his relatively quiet life, experienced what it felt like to be truly furious with someone.

CHAPTER 2

It was in August that construction began at 11 Rollingwood Drive. And the first thing construction would entail was chopping down a large walnut tree that sat near the property line between that house and its neighbor.

"It's a shame it has to go," Oak's mother, Olivia, said with a shake of her head, "but there's nothing to be done about it. If you want to make an omelet, you have to break a few eggs." She said this as Oak stood underneath the tree's wide, green foliage and looked up into its tangle of leaves. The day was hot, but in the circle of the tree's shade, it felt measurably cooler.

Oak did not want the tree to be cut down, but even more than that, she did not want to be moving into this house at all, even when it had a second story added to it, which would be made possible by the clearing of the tree. Besides, the second story was just going to be a master bedroom and bathroom, which wouldn't improve things for Oak at all.

But what Oak wanted did not matter. Her parents insisted that the move was "nonnegotiable."

Not that either of her parents were prone to negotiating, even in the best of circumstances. Take, for example, the time in the fourth grade when Oak had presented them with a detailed presentation about why they should allow her to get a dog. She had given them research about how kids with pets have fewer allergies as adults than kids raised in a pet-free home; she'd showed them studies about how people with dogs live longer and are less depressed than people without dogs; she'd made a chart demonstrating she knew all the responsibilities associated with being a dog owner (feeding, watering, walking, poop scooping, saving allowances toward vet appointments).

But all her mom had said was "We are not dog people, Oak."

And that had been the end of that.

Now they were moving her *here*, to this dumb little house on Rollingwood Drive, which would soon be a not-quite-as-little-but-still-dumb house hundreds of miles from San Francisco, where she'd lived all her life, *here*, to Los Angeles, where it was so hot that people's lawns would dry up and die if they weren't watered on automatic timer systems, where lawn had *no business growing* even.

"You'll feel differently when we're settled in," Mom said, and then she nodded to the man who stood nearby, orange hard hat on his head, chainsaw in his hands.

When the chainsaw growled awake, Oak turned away from the tree and headed back to the car.

Just before she slammed the car door, dulling the sound of the chainsaw, she looked up into the front window of the neighboring house. Peering out at her was a boy with a round white face, flushed red cheeks, a mess of short black curls, and a piercing, angry stare.

"What's *your* problem?" she said out loud, even though he couldn't possibly hear her from inside his house and over the chainsaw's growl.

Later, back at the Residency Suites, where Oak and her mom were staying until the tree was demolished and the master bedroom suite was framed out, Oak lay flat on her back, completely still, on the floor between the two beds. From the bathroom came the sound of her mother taking a shower. Oak crossed her hands on her stomach and felt them rising and falling as she breathed. She stared up at the ceiling, let her eyes run across the vast blankness of it, and tried not to remember everything she had left behind.

The list formed anyway:

- Stacia, her friend since second grade
- Tartine, the bakery around the corner from their old apartment, and their vanilla crème éclairs
- Dolores Park, and basketball games on Saturday mornings with friends
- Rain and cloudy weather
- Wearing sweaters
- Dad

That final one—Dad—wasn't technically something she'd left behind. He'd be driving their stuff down in a few weeks, and though he'd have to go back to San Francisco for work after unloading, it would only be for a couple of months, and then he would join them in Los Angeles.

But the rest of the list was permanent. Maybe Stacia could come visit for a week next summer, or maybe Oak could go stay at her house during spring break, but those maybes were far enough in the future not to count at all.

What bothered Oak more than the loss of any of these things in particular, or all of them collectively, was the fact that neither of her parents cared about what Oak was losing or how she felt about the move.

"Our family isn't a democracy" was the way her mother had put it.

"You can have a vote when you pay the mortgage" was what her father had said.

14

Oak understood that sometimes people had to move because of their parents' jobs. There'd been a kid, Sergio, in her fourth-grade class who'd told them all matter-of-factly that he started almost every year at a new school because of his dad's job as a consultant. It didn't seem like it bothered him at all.

Compared to Sergio, Oak supposed she was lucky. Other than changing apartments when she was three (which she didn't even remember), this was the first time she'd had to move.

And, as Dad had said when Oak complained that it wasn't fair, "Would it be fair to your mom to tell her she can't take this great work opportunity?"

No, Oak had thought, silent but bitter. That wouldn't be fair either. But at least it would be unfair to someone other than her.

Dad had reminded her that he was giving up a lot too, to make this move happen for Mom; he was leaving his job as a graphic designer at First Place Advertising and was going to have to find a new job once he moved down to join them. And he'd be leaving friends, of course, and his favorite coffee shop, which he claimed was "the real tragedy here," as LA didn't "understand coffee" the way the Bay Area did.

"Oak?" Her mother came out of the bathroom. "Where did you go?"

Oak waited a moment before replying. "Down here," she said at last.

Rubbing her head dry with a towel and dressed in her robe, Mom came around the end of the bed and looked down at Oak. "What are you doing down there?"

"Remembering," Oak answered.

"Ah," said Mom, lowering herself to the edge of one of the beds. "Remembering." The towel dropped into her lap, leaving her short, fuzzy hair exposed. It had been nearly two years since her mom had decided to cut her hair so short, practically a buzz, but Oak still missed it. Her mom, on the other hand, said wearing it this way was "freeing," though for the first few months she'd had to wear a hat whenever she went outside to protect the pale white tips of her ears.

The hair had been a big change for her mom, and maybe, Oak thought, looking back, she should have known that it would be the first of many—the hair, then finishing up the master's degree program she'd put on hold years ago when Oak was little. That led to a promotion to project manager at the architecture firm where she worked, and all of that culminated in this most recent, biggest change: a new job at a new firm, with a new title, *junior partner*. Oak should have been proud of her mom, and happy for her.

But she wasn't.

"Oak, baby, I know this is hard for you."

Oak closed her eyes. Her hands, still folded, rose and fell with each breath.

"Change is hard on everyone," Mom went on.

"It isn't hard on *you*," Oak said, eyes still closed.

Mom sighed. Oak imagined her mom rubbing the spot between her eyes the way she often did. Then she said, "I know it might *seem* that way. But change is hard on me, too."

Oak considered opening her eyes, then thought better of it. She rolled onto her side and tucked her hands beneath her head. "I'm tired," she said.

"It's only four o'clock in the afternoon," Mom said, but when Oak did not say anything to this, Mom sighed again. Oak heard the bed shift as her mother stood up and headed to the bathroom. "Twenty minutes," she said. "Then we're going for a walk."

Though Oak had often wished for a pool, after spending over two weeks hanging out at the hotel's, she decided it would be perfectly fine to stay dry for the rest of her life. When the first of September arrived, Oak didn't look back as they drove away from the motel and toward 11 Rollingwood Drive. They arrived to find that the walnut tree had become a stack of firewood in the garage and that the skeleton of what would be the new rooms was attached to the top of the garage.

After depositing their things inside, Oak and her mom waited together on the small front porch for the moving van. There were three good things about this day:

One, Oak wouldn't have to stay in the terrible hotel room any longer.

Two, her stuff from home—the rest of her clothes, her books, the model horse collection that she was too old for but loved anyway—would arrive.

Three, her father would be driving the moving van.

And, Oak thought, watching her mother out of the corner of her eye, she wasn't the only one who was excited to see her dad. Mom had put on lipstick this morning—a deep burgundy red—and she was wearing earrings too, little gold dangly ones with tiny bells.

They were both dressed in cutoff shorts and T-shirts, ready for a day of unpacking, but even so, Mom had put on the earrings and the lipstick. That made Oak feel kind of happy but also sort of embarrassed at the same time.

Without the tree, their front yard and that of their neighbors'—the house where the angry-looking boy had peered out at her through the front window that first day—sort of blended together. Both front yards were mostly grass. The neighbors' house had a bed of flowers that ran along the front underneath the windows, splitting to allow for the path to the front door and then resuming along a small front porch that matched the front porch of Oak's new house.

Between them was the near-flat stump of the decimated walnut tree. And as she studied it, she saw that the grass that had been shaded by its foliage was thinner than the rest of the lawn, probably because it hadn't gotten as much sun. She wondered how long it would take for that circle of grass to grow in as thick as the rest of it, how long before you couldn't tell anymore where the tree had once shaded.

Then Oak saw something that she wasn't sure she saw. Or she didn't see something that she thought she saw. A flicker—a shimmer—right near that tree stump, or maybe just beyond, a movement of light almost as if a mirror had cast and reflected a beam of sun, just there. She squinted her eyes, trying to decide what was casting that strange light.

Just then, a car pulled up into the neighbors' driveway. The driver was a woman with pale skin and strawberry hair. She wore it loose and long, like her skirt. A boy—the one from the other day, the one who had looked so mad—climbed out of the back seat. He was pink cheeked, a little bit round, with moppish dark curls. Together, the boy and his mother gathered grocery bags from the rear of the station wagon.

Maybe she should offer to help, Oak thought. After all, this kid looked about her age, and it would be nice to know someone on the first day of school. . . . She was about to take a step in their direction when she saw that the woman had already collected the final bag.

The kid slammed shut the trunk, and he followed his mom up the path to their front door. But before they went inside, both the woman and the boy turned to look at Oak and her mother. Oak started to raise her hand to wave hello, but then the woman tightened her lips into a straight line. Slowly, she shook her head—at Oak? at her mother?—and then turned to unlock the door.

The boy did the same thing; he shook his head at her. Suddenly Oak felt glad she hadn't offered to help.

"Did you see that?" Oak's mother said. "How rude!"

It *was* rude. Oak's hand, which she had been prepared to wave, tightened into a fist instead.

CHAPTER 3

Having set his share of groceries in the kitchen, Alder retreated to his bedroom, where he watched the new neighbors.

He was watching even though it felt remarkably like *spying*, something he knew his mother wouldn't approve of. Alder and his mother were both fans of privacy, and Alder had always known that the price of privacy was granting others privacy in return.

Still, he found he couldn't look away from the girl and her mother, who stood together on the front porch next door waiting, it seemed, for something.

He told himself that it was their own fault that he was watching them; if they hadn't cut down the beautiful walnut tree, he wouldn't have had nearly as good a view. And oh, that tree. It had been much older than Alder, already a giant before he was born. It seemed so cruel to kill a giant. And his mother agreed. When she had seen what the new neighbors had done, she had looked for a moment as if she would cry. His mom was something of a crier; a goofy commercial for homeowners' insurance that featured a family weathering a storm together could find her bursting into tears; if the mood struck her just right, even the beginning of the commercial's jingle could get her going, so Alder had gotten good at grabbing the clacker and switching the channel at the very first notes of that particular ad.

She cried when she was happy; she cried when she was sad. She cried sometimes listening to Canary's music. She cried when Alder gave her a picture he had painted of Mort when he was in the third grade. So the day the tree had been cut down, Alder had expected his mom to cry.

But she hadn't. Though her eyes reddened and her mouth stiffened and her nostrils flared, Alder's mother hadn't cried. Instead, she'd said just two words:

"That woman."

Then she'd turned and gone to her bedroom, and she'd closed the door softly.

After his mom had closed herself in her room, Alder had visited the portrait of his family. There he was as a baby; there were his parents; there was the tree. If they were to try to take another photo now, it would be just Alder and his mom standing in front of a stump. No more tree. No more Dad.

As Alder watched the girl and the woman through his bedroom window, he thought about the way his mom had said those words. *That woman.*

Then there was the rumble of a truck and the honk of a horn, and a moving van—not a professional one but the kind that people rent to move their own stuff—pulled up in front of 11 Rollingwood Drive, and the girl's face broke into a wide happy smile, bright as sunshine. She took off at a run down to the curb.

The truck's driver got out and picked her up and swung her around in a wide happy arc. *That woman* joined them at the curb, and the man—the girl's father, Alder suspected—put the girl down. He turned to the woman and hugged her tight, lifted her off her feet, and swung her around too, and then he kissed her on the mouth.

Alder turned away. *Enough of that*, he told himself.

School started the following Monday—sixth grade at Golden Key Elementary, the same school Alder had attended since kindergarten.

This year, he'd gotten lucky. Mr. Rivera would be his teacher. Mr. Rivera was everyone's favorite. He was known to be funny and he liked practical jokes, both those he played and those played on him, and Alder couldn't wait to share his prank idea with his friend Marcus.

So Alder woke up that morning in a particularly good mood, and he hummed over his oatmeal, and he packed his backpack with pencils and pens and notebooks and the sheet of googly eyes and the little tin of false mustaches. Marcus would laugh hysterically when Alder told him the plan—to decorate all the classroom's posters with the googly eyes and the mustaches. Alder barely stopped to say goodbye to his mom before he rushed off to the bus stop.

Marcus would already be on the bus; his house was three stops before Alder's.

It was a beautiful day—as hot as summer still. Though fall was just around the corner, there was a difference to the quality of light that signaled it was time to go back to school. The deciduous trees' leaves were dry at the edges, beginning to transition to oranges and yellows, and though it was still a ways off, Alder began to imagine what Halloween would be like this year. Was sixth grade too old to wear a costume, or trick-or-treat? He didn't think so, but maybe he'd check with Marcus to see what his thoughts were.

It had been a month or so since he and Marcus had actually talked, because Marcus had dropped his phone in the toilet and his parents had decided that he'd have to wait until his next birthday, all the way in April, to get a replacement. Also, Marcus had signed up for the cross-country club, and Alder guessed that getting into shape for that was probably taking lots of Marcus's time. That was something Alder had no interest in, at all—sports in general, and running in particular. Apparently, that's all cross-country was. Running, for a long time.

But that was the thing about friends, Alder thought happily. You didn't actually have to have a lot in common with someone to be their friend. After all, he and Marcus were pretty different if you thought about it: Marcus had a big family with two parents and four siblings, while Alder's family was just him and his mom; Marcus was into sports, and Alder was into knitting—a hobby Marcus *loved* to tease him about; Marcus had lots of friends and Alder did not. Marcus talked to everyone—before class, at lunch, during recess, after school.

They'd been friends for so long that probably those differences didn't mean much. Alder had known Marcus since the first grade. He had been there the day that Marcus broke his wrist when he fell from the climbing structure at the park. Marcus had cheered Alder up that time he'd gotten that horrible haircut. And he and Marcus were comfortable together; they knew things like where to find extra toilet paper at each other's houses. He wondered if Marcus's family still kept it where they used to—in the cabinet under the sink all the way to the right.

Maybe, Alder admitted to himself as he walked up the block to wait for the bus, he was a little bit more Marcus's friend than Marcus was his friend. Marcus could have come by Alder's house some day after running with the rest of the kids in the club, or he could have asked his mom to call Alder's mom to see if they could hang out. But Marcus had been busy. That was okay; because Alder was his friend, he understood. Besides, they'd get to hang out a lot now that school was starting again.

Alder grinned, imagining Marcus's face when he saw the mustaches and the googly eyes.

The bus arrived right on time, and there was Faith, the same driver from last year, grinning down at him as she opened the door.

"Hiya, Alder," she said. "Welcome aboard." That was what she always said.

"Hiya, Faith," Alder answered as he mounted the steps, which was what almost every kid said in reply.

The year was off to a comfortable start, Alder thought comfortably. He turned down the bus's aisle, looking for Marcus and the seat he always saved for Alder. And there was Marcus, five rows back on the left.

But there was no empty seat beside him.

Instead, there was Beck Taylor.

It's no big deal, Alder told himself as he made his way down the aisle. *Maybe Marcus told him he could sit there just until my stop.*

He stopped alongside Marcus and Beck's bench. "Hey, Marcus," he said. "Hey, Beck."

Beck grinned back at him, his face sunburned and ruddy. "Hey, Alder," he said.

Marcus raised his chin in Alder's direction. "What's up," he said, but it wasn't really a question.

"Um," said Alder. "Guess what. I mean, I brought—" He swung his backpack around to his front and unzipped it, feeling around for the mustache tin.

"Train's pulling out of the station," Faith called from the driver's seat. "Have a seat, Alder!"

"It's in here somewhere, I'll find it in a second," Alder muttered, glancing at Marcus. "It's the stuff for the prank."

"What prank?" Marcus asked. Not in a mean voice— just as if he truly didn't remember. Which, Alder thought, his hand dropping away from his backpack, was even worse.

"Dude, look at this one," Beck said, nudging Marcus. He was watching a surfing video on the small screen of his phone, and Marcus turned his attention to it.

"Awesome," Marcus said.

Alder trudged down the aisle and slumped into an empty row near the very back of the bus. Faith pulled the bus onto the road and they headed off toward school, toward what suddenly felt like unknown territory to Alder.

It should have made Alder feel better that Mr. Rivera started off the school day with a prank: he'd turned all the desks toward the back of the room, lined up in neat rows just as they should be, but facing in the wrong direction, away from the whiteboard.

Everyone laughed, and there were screeches and scratches as desks were turned right way around, as everyone settled into seats.

"You can sit where you want for now," Mr. Rivera said loudly, over all the rearranging sounds, "but if you guys start to get out of control, we'll have to assign seats."

Mr. Rivera used "we" in the same way most grown-ups did: not to indicate the group as a whole, but rather to speak of himself.

"The royal *we*," his mother called it. "Also known as the majestic plural."

Mr. Rivera's use of the majestic plural did not bode as well for the coming year as the turned-around desks did.

The desk next to Marcus was open, but the one on his other side was taken by Beck, and they were talking loudly about some weekend surfing trip up the coast the two of them had taken with Beck's family, something Alder hadn't known had happened. Apparently they had been spending lots of time together this summer.

Alder could have sat on the other side of Marcus, but instead he took a desk in the front row, close to a window, and turned it to face the front of the room.

"Okay, gang," Mr. Rivera said, grinning at them. He had a friendly face—a bushy dark mustache, brown skin and eyes, black hair that flopped over his forehead. He wore a tie, one unlike any ties Alder had seen before; it seemed to be knit out of yarn, and it was skinny and squared off at the bottom. His shoes, Alder noticed, were loafers with actual pennies inserted into the slots on the front.

"Most of you know each other, but I don't know all of you just yet," Mr. Rivera said. He went to his desk and picked up a stack of name tag stickers and began counting out five per row, handing them to the kids at the front desks to pass back. Alder took the stack, kept the top name tag, and passed the rest to Cynthia Chen, who sat behind him. "I'm pretty good at names, but not great, so if you'll all do me the favor of writing down your first name on one of these babies and wearing them for the rest of the day, dollars to doughnuts I'll have your names memorized by the last bell."

"Do we get doughnuts if you don't know our names by then?" called out Beck, and the class laughed.

"Sure, why not," Mr. Rivera said. "But if I *do* know them, you owe *me* a doughnut, how about that?"

"All right," Beck agreed, and immediately students started whispering plans to one another to sway the odds in their doughnut direction:

"Write your name really small so he can't read it!"

"Wear your tag upside down!"

"Use pencil instead of pen! That makes it harder to see!"

Mr. Rivera chuckled and smiled, and he didn't shush them.

Alder wrote his name in little tiny letters, then peeled the backing from the name tag and stuck it to his chest just above his heart.

Mr. Rivera really *was* cool, Alder thought. This made him feel a bit better, even if he wasn't sitting next to Marcus.

Then the classroom door opened.

"Excuse me?" came a voice. Everyone's head swiveled to see who it was.

Alder froze. It was the girl. Alder's new neighbor.

"I'm new here?" said the girl like it was a question. "I'm sorry I'm late."

"Welcome," said Mr. Rivera. "Come on in, take a seat. Here's a name tag."

The girl took the tag from Mr. Rivera's outstretched hand and looked around the room. There was an empty desk one row over and one seat back from where Alder sat.

She took it.

"Write your name really small," Cynthia whispered to the new girl. She nodded, took out a green marker, and did as Cynthia had told her without even asking why.

Pretending to look for something in his backpack, Alder turned around and stole a glance at the girl's name tag as she stuck it on her shirt. She'd made the letters tiny; Alder squinted to read them.

Oak, the name tag read.

"A funny name for a tree killer," Alder muttered.

But the words came out more loudly than he'd meant them to, and the girl heard him, her wide eyes meeting his. She looked surprised for a moment, like he'd caught her off guard, but then she narrowed her gaze.

"So you're the creeper who keeps watching me out his window," Oak said, and her voice rang loudly so the whole class could hear her—no accident, Alder knew.

He turned quickly back around, feeling his cheeks flame red. *That girl*, Alder thought to himself, his voice in his head echoing the exact tone in which his mother had said *That woman*.

It was only 9:17 in the morning. And already, the day felt ruined.

CHAPTER 4

Until today, Oak had spent every school day in the same building—a kindergarten-through-sixth-grade Montessori school that had been just around the way from her house.

Her *old* house, Oak reminded herself.

She'd never given much thought to the school, just as she'd never given much thought to her house—actually, her apartment, a first-floor flat in a three-story purple row house. Painted Ladies, they were called, those colorful San Francisco homes. That was something else she'd taken for granted—how colorful all the buildings had been back home. Here, most of the houses were beige stucco, and if an occasional door was painted a bright color, it was almost always red.

This school was no different—the stucco painted a darker brown than most of the surrounding houses, but that was all. The kids seemed all right, for the most part . . . that weird creepo boy from next door was in her class, so that wasn't great, but Mr. Rivera was pretty funny, and the girl at the desk next to her, Cynthia Chen, seemed like a good potential friend.

It was a little weird to be confined to one desk for so much of the day. Back home in the Montessori school, kids had been free to move around as much as they wanted, taking their work to the classroom's back table if they wanted to spread out, or to slump in a beanbag, or even to head outdoors and read under a tree if the day was nice. There had been a cat that visited the school from time to time, meandering through the schoolyard and occasionally napping on someone's lap if they were sitting still. Oak had always sat as still as possible, even if her legs fell asleep.

She had often thought how nice it would be if the cat had followed her home one day after school, but it never did. Sometimes it visited the school every day, and sometimes it disappeared for weeks at a time, but it always came back around eventually. Now, Oak realized with a start, *she* was the one who had disappeared. Even though she'd never known the cat's name, and even though the cat hadn't seemed particularly fond of Oak—no fonder than it was of any other warm lap—she felt terribly guilty that she'd left without saying goodbye.

Oak's mom had packed her a lunch, but she walked by the paid lunch line in the cafeteria to check it out and it didn't look awful; there was pizza, even. Maybe she'd see if her mom would let her bring money tomorrow.

But today, Oak took her bagged lunch from her backpack and stood awkwardly near the edge of the cafeteria. There were seats inside, but there was also a set of large, heavy doors to a patio outside, and these were pushed open. A bright rectangle of sunlight beckoned.

It *was* bright out there, and Oak felt suddenly vulnerable, as if she had been thrust onto a stage without her lines, and she blinked against the blinding light.

"Hey!" called a girl's voice. "Oak! Come sit with us."

Oak's eyes adjusted, and she looked around. There, at a nearby picnic bench, was Cynthia, a sandwich in hand, waving.

There were three other girls at Cynthia's table, and Cynthia introduced Oak to each of them as she threaded her legs over the bench and sat down.

"Oak," Cynthia said, touching the arm of the girl who sat between her and Oak, "this is Miriam. She's in our class."

"Hi," Oak said, feeling shy.

"And that's Cameron and Carmen," Cynthia said, waving her sandwich at the girls who sat across the table. "They're twins."

Oak almost said, "No way," in a sarcastic voice, but she stopped herself just in time and instead said only, "It's nice to meet you."

"Hello," said the twin on the left.

"Hello," said the twin on the right.

"I'm sorry," Oak said, "but which of you is Cameron and which is Carmen?"

"I'm Carmen," said the twin on the left, and Oak noticed that the pizza slice on her plate was pepperoni, while the pizza slice on Cameron's plate was plain cheese.

Oak opened her bag and pulled out her sandwich—cheese and tomato—and an apple, and a little bag of chips.

"So, where'd you move from?" Cameron asked.

"San Francisco."

"Ooh," said Miriam brightly, "I love Frisco! We went last summer. Are all those seals still on that wharf?"

Oak closed her eyes for a long moment. *No one* who actually knew San Francisco would call it "Frisco." But she decided to let it pass. "Probably," she said, answering the question Miriam had asked about seals; in fact, they were sea lions, a whole mess of them that lived at Pier 39, a favorite attraction of tourists. "I mean, they usually are." Actually, they *always* were.

"They're so cute," Miriam said. "Do you know their names?"

"Whose names?"

"The *seals'* names."

Was this girl serious? "They're actually sea lions," Oak said. "Not seals."

"O-oh," said Miriam, nodding. "I always mix those up. Like alligators and crocodiles."

"What's the difference between an alligator and a crocodile?" Carmen asked.

Cameron answered, "One you'll see later, the other you'll see after a while."

It took Oak half a second to get the joke, and then it struck her as ridiculously funny. She laughed—a sharp, loud bray of a laugh. The sound made the other girls laugh, too, and they laughed wildly together. By the time they all calmed down, just a minute or so later, they were friends.

"So," Mom said, when she arrived at the end of the day to collect Oak from school, "how was it?"

"It was good," Oak said, shoving her backpack into the rear seat of the car and then following it inside. Buckling her seat belt, Oak caught her mother's eye in the rearview mirror. Her mother looked a little too smug. "I mean," Oak said, "it was all right. It could have been worse."

"Well," Mom said, "that's almost always true."

Oak didn't know what to say to that. She rolled down her window and let the wind tangle her hair. The sun warmed her face. Whether or not she wanted to admit it, she did like how warm it was here. San Francisco was a damp place, foggy and cool. Here in Los Angeles, the air was not only warmer but also drier.

"Tomorrow," Mom said a few minutes later as they pulled onto Rollingwood Drive, "you can ride the bus to school. There's a stop just here, at the corner." She slowed down and waved her hand to indicate where the bus would pick Oak up.

"Okay," she said. There was no use arguing about it; just like the move, taking the bus seemed to have been decided without asking what *she* wanted. "Do you even miss home a little?" Oak asked, resentful.

Mom pulled the car up to the curb in front of their new house. She couldn't park in the driveway because that's where the construction workers had set up their tools and scaffolding. Three of them clambered around in the framework they'd erected, tossing scraps of fluffy pink insulation material into the dumpster in the driveway. Only two of them, Oak noticed, were wearing hard hats. The third guy had on a baseball cap.

Mom didn't get out of the car right away. "I thought you knew," she said, "I grew up not far from here. I didn't move to the Bay Area until I was an adult."

This was news to Oak, and she sat very still, waiting to see if Mom would share anything else. Mom wasn't a big fan of talking about her childhood; usually when Oak asked anything, her mom would say, "The past is in the past."

But instead of talking, Mom pulled the key from the ignition and climbed out of the car. "Hey," she called up to the construction guys, "you! Put your hard hat back on."

"Yes, boss," the guy answered with a grin, saluting Oak's mom.

Oak got out of the car too. She slung her backpack over her shoulder and headed into the house.

Her mom had done a lot of unpacking while Oak had been at school; six or seven boxes, flattened and stacked, leaned against the wall just inside the front door. Most of them were labeled "Kitchen," which hopefully meant that the next time Oak reached for her favorite mug—the green one with a frog's face—it would be there.

Grudgingly, Oak admitted to herself that the place was beginning to feel a little bit like home. The brown leather L-shaped couch made the area in front of the fireplace feel like an actual room, and before he'd left, Dad had installed their flat-screen TV above the fireplace. Right now, one of Mom's playlists was on, the one she liked to listen to while doing chores. The lamps were unpacked—both of the clear glass table lamps, one tall and thin, the other squat and fat, with matching burlap shades, and the standing lamp too, a knobby mahogany base with a shade made out of woven sticks. The bookshelves were up too, and it looked like Mom had begun to sort the books that would go on them but had given up midway through the first box, which sat opened on the floor in front of the shelves.

Oak didn't have any homework since it was just the first day of school, so she let her backpack fall to the rug near the front door and headed over to the bookshelf boxes.

Mom, Oak observed, had opened the box labeled "Fiction," which, Oak thought, was as good a place as any to begin.

Most of the books in this box Oak had never read; they were grown-up books about marriage and jobs and mysteries that held no interest for her, that felt, the few times she'd thumbed through one of them, to be so far off as to be more fictional than the most magical of fairy tales. There was one book, shorter than the others, and without a dust jacket. Its cover was black and its title, *Feline Teleportation*, was gold embossed down the spine.

Though Oak had never read this book, she had a fondness for it; her father had brought it home from a business trip he'd taken to Seattle several years ago and had given it to her mother.

"It was the strangest shop," Oak's dad had told her mom. "Full of weird things. I mean, this book was one of the most normal things there."

Suddenly, Oak had an idea. What if, instead of

organizing the books by category—fiction, nonfiction, kids' books—she were to organize them instead by *color*? She could arrange them in a rainbow, with red books on the highest shelf, and working her way down, shelf by shelf and left to right, until the purple-spined books ended the rainbow on the bottom right corner of the shelf.

It was a great plan. "Mom," she called into the kitchen, where she could hear her banging around, "are these all the book boxes?"

"There might be a couple more in the corner of the dining room," Mom called back. "I didn't realize how many books we had! We might need to donate some."

There they were. Three boxes, one labeled "Cookbooks" and the other two labeled "Books, Misc.," stacked in a corner. Oak dragged the boxes one by one, too heavy to lift, into the front room and set to work.

CHAPTER 5

Sometimes, when Alder was the saddest, he would wait until his mom was distracted, and then he would move a kitchen chair across the room and up against the bookshelf, and he would very carefully lift Mort down. Walking quickly but quietly, Alder would take the stuffed opossum to his room, shut his door for privacy, and hold him.

This was exactly what Alder did when he got home from the first day of sixth grade, following the second bus ride of the day in which he didn't sit next to Marcus —not because he was sitting next to someone else but because Marcus wasn't on the bus at all, but rather off on a run with the cross-country club. His mother had left a note saying that she was at an exercise class and would be home soon, so when Alder found himself alone, he went to the kitchen for a chair and climbed up to retrieve the opossum.

Holding Mort, Alder sat on his bed, on the quilt that was still rumpled from last night's sleep. Out the front window, he could see the sad, nearly flat stump, all that was left of the walnut tree. Alder didn't like to look at the stump. Gently, he placed one hand on the opossum's back. The fur felt comfortably soft, softer than it looked.

Mort's feet were affixed to a smoothly polished, asymmetrical piece of driftwood. He stood as if at alert, his belly raised up from the wood, his four legs spread heroically apart. His mouth tilted upward in a mysterious smile, not unlike the smile of the Mona Lisa, which Alder had seen pictures of in his history textbook at school.

Unlike the Mona Lisa, Mort's teeth were exposed by his smile—not all of them, but a few sharp top teeth. A tiny tip of his pink tongue stuck out just a bit, but Alder didn't think the tongue was real. Maybe it was made of plastic, or rubber.

Mort's coat was mottled brown and black and cream. His front legs were covered in short dark fur, and the back legs were hairier, the same mixture of long, multicolored fur as his body. Mort's face, around his pink nose and black whiskers, was white, except for a darker patch between his eyes that extended up between his black rounded ears and over the back of his head, joining with the mottled fur of the rest of his coat. His toes were pink and hairless. His tail, curved perpetually in a C shape that veered to the left, was dark at the base and then yellowish-white to the tip, not unlike the tail of a rat, only bigger.

Except for the fact that he was perpetually attached to a piece of wood and the fact that he was perfectly still—not really *dead*, since he couldn't rot and didn't smell, but definitely not *alive*, either, in spite of the fact that he stood on his feet and his eyes were open—Mort looked exactly as Alder expected any opossum would look.

And Alder knew it was a little weird that he liked to hold the opossum, which was why he did it so infrequently, and why he closed his bedroom door. Still, he *did* like it. It made him feel . . . a little more solid, somehow, the way Mort was made more solid by his base of driftwood.

He sat in his bedroom with Mort on his lap for a good long while. He waited until he heard Mom get home and run a bath, which she did sometimes after an exercise class. Soon after that he stood up and headed to the living room to return Mort to his rightful place well before he figured Mom would be done washing up.

But maybe he misjudged the time and spent too long in his room, or maybe Mom had just taken an unusually short bath, because when Alder and Mort emerged from his bedroom, it was to find Mom sitting on the pink couch, waiting.

The kitchen chair was right where Alder had left it, up

43

against the bookshelf. Alder climbed atop it, carefully put Mort back where he belonged, and then climbed down again.

"Hey, buddy," Mom said, and she patted the spot beside her.

It was weird, Alder thought, that he could both want to do something and not want to do something at exactly the same time, the way he both wanted to and didn't want to sit next to his mom. There must be a word for that, he thought. Maybe he would ask Mr. Rivera.

He did go over to the couch and sit next to his mom, but not quite as close as where she had patted. Even so, she wrapped one arm around him and pulled him toward her, and after a moment's resistance, Alder rested his cheek on the fabric of his mom's white T-shirt, on her shoulder. Her hair, still damp, tickled the back of his neck.

They sat there together for a few minutes, not talking. The big front window was orange and bright with the setting sun; without the foliage of the walnut tree to filter the sun's rays, it looked almost like the whole thing was trying to get inside, to be with Alder and his mom. It was so brightly beautiful that Alder had to close his eyes against it, but even then he could see the brightness through the closed lids of his eyes, he could feel its warmth on his face, magnified through the window glass.

But eventually, the sun slipped away. Alder could tell when the light behind his eyes grew dimmer, when the warmth on his skin faded, and then he opened his eyes.

Mom squeezed him once more and kissed his head. "I love you, kiddo," she said.

"I love you, too," Alder mumbled, pulling away.

Mom stood up, ran her hands down the front of her jeans. "Come on," she said. "I've got an idea."

Dinner was chili, already simmering in the slow cooker, but Mom said it could wait. She grabbed her purse and her keys from the counter and headed for the car. Alder followed.

"Where are we going?" he asked, slamming into the back seat.

"I've been thinking about it for a while," Mom said, "and tonight seems like just the right night to do it."

"Do *what*?" Alder felt his heart thumping with excitement. Every now and then, his mom surprised him with some wild thing, like a weekend trip to the San Diego Zoo last spring, or that time a year ago when she'd driven him and Marcus to an orchard for apple picking one day after school, followed by big mugs of steaming cider.

"You'll see," Mom said, and she caught his eyes in the rearview mirror and grinned. "Don't worry," she said. "It's a good surprise."

Alder wasn't worried. Mom's surprises were always good. And thinking about what the good surprise could be filled him with bubbles, bubbles that rose and burst and popped, taking up all the room that had been filled with sadness, before, and embarrassment about being caught with Mort.

It was just dark enough for their headlights to glow in front of them, and their light swept the road in front of the car as Mom drove up Rollingwood Drive to the corner and took a right. Then, at the main intersection, she headed left.

What was in this direction? Alder tried to remember. There was the grocery store; maybe they were going for ice cream. But that didn't seem to be nearly a big enough surprise for the way his mom was acting.

There was the roller rink. That could be it, Alder supposed. Maybe they were going roller skating. If that was the surprise, Alder would be disappointed, though he promised himself that he wouldn't let Mom know it was a disappointment, since she was such a fan of roller skating.

But, to his relief, they drove right past the roller rink.

Then Mom put on the left blinker and waited for traffic to clear so that she could pull into a shopping center. Alder craned his neck to see what shops were in the center: there was a coffee shop, and a dry cleaner's, and a yoga studio . . .

And a pet store.

Mom pulled her car up in front of the store and parked it. She turned around and grinned. "What do you think?" she said. "Want to meet some kittens?"

✳ ⭐ ✳

The big glass door of the pet shop had a sign affixed to it:

CAT ADOPTION FAIR ALL WEEK!

"I saw the sign earlier, when I was picking up the dry cleaning," Mom said, as the glass doors slid open to reveal a brightly lit store stocked with aisles of pet care products, a section to the left for dog stuff, a section to the right for cat supplies. "And I didn't think too much of it at the time, but . . ." Mom cleared her throat before continuing, "Well, you're a sixth grader now. You're old enough for some responsibility, don't you think?"

"I almost killed the fern," Alder admitted, hesitant to remind his mom of that fact in case she changed her mind, but compelled to be truthful anyway.

"Oh, that," she said. "Plants are hard to keep alive. They don't meow at you when they're thirsty."

That was an excellent point.

"Also," Alder said, "I'm older now." And he headed to the kitten adoption area.

"Much older," Mom agreed, following behind.

The kittens were together in a hexagon-shaped enclosure, an olive-skinned young woman standing nearby. She wore her dark hair in a long braid, and she had two badges affixed to her yellow blouse, one that read "Volunteer" and another that read "Rosa." When Alder leaned into the enclosure to get a closer look at the kittens, she said in a friendly voice, "Hi! Are you thinking about adopting today?"

"Yes," Mom said, and that made it seem 100 percent real. Alder grinned up at the young woman, and she grinned back.

"They're all sweethearts," she told him. "Would you like to go inside with them?"

"Can I?" Alder asked, and the young woman answered by unlatching the small gate and pulling it open.

He walked through quickly so none of the kittens—there were five of them—could escape, and then he folded his legs and sat down on the ground.

Three of the kittens came over to him right away: a black kitten with a thick black tail held up proudly like a paintbrush and two orange-and-white-striped kittens that looked like they could be twins.

The other two kittens, a gray one and a calico, didn't look all that interested in meeting Alder; one was asleep on a cushion, and the other was seriously concentrated on a dish of kibble.

The two orange kittens and the black one clambered up on his legs, mewing and purring and butting his hands with their heads. Alder laughed at how cute they were.

"They sure like you," the young woman said, and Alder looked up to see Mom smiling down at him.

He opened his mouth to speak, but before he could ask, Mom said, "Only one, Alder," and she sounded like she meant it.

In the end, Alder chose the smaller of the two orange kittens. Of the three that had approached him, this one, he figured, was the one who most needed a home. Maybe she was small because the other kittens pushed her out of the way and took most of the kibble; maybe, back home, she'd get nice and fat if she didn't have to compete for food.

The young woman put the small orange kitten in a cardboard carrier; it had air holes poked in it, so Alder knew his kitten was fine, but even so, he wished he could just take her out and carry her in his arms.

He held the box while his mom shopped for the essentials—food and a litter box and litter—and he filled out as much information as he could on the adoption paperwork. His name, Alder Madigan, their address, 15 Rollingwood Drive, his mom's phone number.

There was a line near the top that read "Name of Pet." Thinking of the plant back home, Alder wrote, in firm, clear letters, "Fern."

"That's a great name," the young woman said. "I'm sure you'll give Fern a very good home."

Mom returned from shopping for kitten supplies and signed the adoption paperwork, smiling when she saw what Alder had named the kitten. "And don't worry," the lady said. "I'll bet someone will be in any day now to adopt her brother."

"Her brother? The other orange one?"

She nodded. "They were found together, in a dumpster. Littermates."

"Oh," Alder said, and his joy felt punctured now, at the thought of separating Fern from her brother. He looked up to his mom, wondering if this news—that the two orange kittens were siblings—might sway her decision to take home just a single kitten.

But no. "I'm sure he'll find a wonderful home," Mom said. "I'm sure they all will."

And so Alder had no choice but to pick up the cardboard carrier with Fern inside and follow Mom back toward the car.

Fern's brother, he told himself, buckling into the back seat and cradling the box on his lap, holding it carefully as his mom turned on the headlights and backed out of the parking space, would be just fine.

CHAPTER 6

The next morning, Oak walked up the street to the corner where her mom had told her the bus would come to collect her. She left a little bit early, just to be safe, and there was a touch of something that felt like fall in the air. Back home in San Francisco, the days would be cool already, and feeling this colder air made Oak especially homesick.

She sighed deeply and stopped on the corner. There was no one else there, and after a few minutes, Oak wondered if maybe she'd misunderstood her mother, or if perhaps her mother had been wrong. But then she saw someone else walking up Rollingwood Drive toward her: her next-door neighbor and classmate. *Alder*, his name tag had read. She was relieved to see him, even though she didn't like him, because his presence meant that she was in the right place after all.

He didn't look thrilled to see *her*, and other than lifting his chin a tiny bit in acknowledgment of her presence, he didn't say hello, and his hands stayed where they were, firmly holding on to the straps of his backpack.

They stood there, side by side, waiting for the bus without talking. Finally, though, Oak thought, *This is ridiculous*, and said, "So, do you think Mr. Rivera will bring us doughnuts today?"

For a second, it seemed like Alder was going to ignore her, but he must have decided that was *too* rude, because he answered. "Why would he? He learned all our names by the end of the day."

Oak shrugged. "I dunno, but I'll bet he does. He just seems like the kind of guy who would."

"Whatever," Alder said. "I'll bet he doesn't."

"Then it's a bet," Oak challenged, annoyed by what a jerk Alder was being. What did he have against her, anyway? *He* was the weird window creeper, not her!

"Whatever," Alder said again.

Just then, the bus arrived.

"Five dollars," Oak threw over her shoulder as the bus doors opened and she mounted the first step.

Alder didn't reply.

"Well, *you're* new," said the driver. She was a pale, youngish woman with short brown hair that lay in a wave across her forehead. Her ears were each pierced three times, and she wore a black T-shirt with white block letters that read "THE TRUTH IS OUT THERE" and jeans with holes in the knees and black lace-up boots. Oak immediately decided she liked her.

"I'm Faith," the bus driver said. "What's your name?"

"Oak," said Oak.

Faith's eyebrows shot up in surprise. "No kidding," she said. "How about that? Two tree kids on one street."

Oak felt offended to have been lumped in with Alder, but she decided to forgive Faith this one time.

But as she walked down the aisle, Faith called after her, "Two tree kids! On one street called *Rollingwood*!"

She would have to forgive Faith twice.

Mr. Rivera greeted the class with not one, not two, but *three* boxes of doughnuts.

"Regular, gluten free, and vegan," he said proudly. "Everyone, take one to start."

The line for the regular box was longest, so Oak decided to try a vegan doughnut. Cynthia was in that line ahead of her.

"Oh!" said Cynthia. "Are you vegan, too?"

"No," Oak said, "but I don't mind eating like one."

"Meat is murder," Cynthia said wisely.

"I guess," Oak said, though she thought "murder" was maybe taking it a bit far. "Are *you* a vegan?"

"Most of the time," Cynthia said. She selected a maple bar and placed it on a napkin. Oak took a round glazed.

It felt weird to sit back down in rows to eat the doughnuts; it seemed like everyone felt like doughnuts turned the classroom into a semi-party, and people clumped together in groups of threes and fours, turning toward each other so their backs were out to the rest of the room.

Oak clustered up with Cynthia and Miriam. Miriam had taken one of the gluten-free doughnuts, chocolate with chocolate frosting. It was smaller than the regular doughnuts and it looked denser.

Oak glanced around at the other clusters as she bit into her doughnut; there was a really tall, athletic-looking boy with floppy blond hair and a sunburn, laughing with a group of boys around him. It was the biggest group, six boys all together. There was a clutch of four girls over by the window at the front of the classroom, laughing conspiratorially about something. There were a few boys and one girl over by the door, talking about a game, it sounded like, from the scrap of conversation Oak overheard.

"That game really plays best if you have a couple of icosahedrons," one of the boys said.

The girl who was with them, who wore her straight black hair in a ponytail laced through the hole in the back of her baseball cap, rolled her eyes behind thick purple frames and said, "Just call it a d-twenty, Dorian—no one is impressed." Her name was Darla; Oak remembered from her name tag the day before.

Mr. Rivera stood, leaning on his desk, ankles crossed, smiling as he chewed. His mustache, Oak noticed, was dusted with powdered sugar. When he'd popped the last piece into his mouth, he wiped the sugar from his face, balled up the napkin, and threw it overhand toward the trash can. It missed by at least a foot, landing soundlessly on the floor.

Mr. Rivera looked up and saw that Oak had seen his bad shot. He smiled and shrugged, like *What can you do?* and then retrieved the napkin and tossed it in the can.

She liked him, Oak decided. Doughnuts, and a sense of humor, and plus he'd earned her five dollars. Oak looked around the room, wondering where Alder was; maybe she could collect her winnings now and rub it in a little.

But then she saw him—he was sitting alone at his desk and picking forlornly at a doughnut. Oak suddenly didn't feel like being pushy or making fun.

"Okay, kiddos, finish up your doughnuts," Mr. Rivera said. "It's time to get to work!"

The class broke into a collective groan, but Alder, Oak noticed, looked relieved. He folded a napkin around his doughnut and tucked it into his desk, then reached around into his backpack to get out his school stuff.

The other kids filed toward the trash can to throw

away their napkins; the sunburned kid, Oak noticed, and another boy, who seemed to be his friend—Marcus, she thought his name was—both successfully tossed in their balled-up napkins from a pretty impressive distance, causing Mr. Rivera to whistle in appreciation. Within a few minutes, everyone was seated at their desks, and they had to pull out their science books, and the school day began.

"I want to try something a little different this year," Mr. Rivera said. "Something exciting."

Oak didn't know how exciting anything he had planned could be, if it had to do with the heavy brick of a textbook on her desk, but she was willing to listen.

"Each of us is made of many pieces," Mr. Rivera began, snapping off the cap from a green marker and turning to the whiteboard. "Let's make a list."

He wrote in big block letters, all capitals:

PIECES OF A PERSON

"Arms!" shouted out Marcus, and the class erupted into laughter.

Mr. Rivera laughed too. "Sure," he said, "arms." And he wrote it on the board, followed by another word—BODIES.

"Okay," he continued, "so we don't have to list all the parts of the human body one by one, because that could take all day, let's just leave it at BODIES. And, yes! We are made of our bodies. But what else?"

There was a moment when no one said anything, and Mr. Rivera stood patiently waiting, twirling the green marker around his fingers in a smooth and practiced motion.

Then Cynthia said, "Memories?"

"Yes!" said Mr. Rivera. "Definitely."

MEMORIES went on the board underneath ARMS—BODIES.

"Family," someone yelled from the back.

Mr. Rivera nodded and added FAMILY to the list.

The class seemed to loosen up, and kids called out words almost as fast as Mr. Rivera could write.

"DNA!"

"Water!"

"Blood!"

"Traditions!"

"Love."

"Electricity."

"Teeth!"

"Toenails!"

"Bacteria! We're made of millions of them!"

Mr. Rivera wrote down each contribution, including the body parts, even though he'd said they'd lump those together. Soon the board was covered in an assortment of words that looked pretty strange together.

"Okay," Mr. Rivera said at last, capping his marker and setting it aside. "Now, I want you all to copy down this list, and I want you to circle three of these things, whichever seem the most interesting to you."

Oak used capital block letters to write her list, like Mr. Rivera had. Then she sat back and stared at the words. Which ones intrigued her the most?

Slowly, she circled ELECTRICITY.

Then, MEMORIES.

And finally, FAMILY.

CHAPTER 7

TOENAILS
WATER
FAMILY

Those were the three words that Alder circled from his list. Water, because he knew how important it was for life—the fern's near-death experience had made sure he'd never forget that; family, because Alder barely had any—it was just him and his mom, the smallest size a family could be; and toenails, because that was the most ridiculous thing on the list, and Alder couldn't help himself.

"Okay," Mr. Rivera said after everyone had circled their three words. "Now, who remembers what subject we're supposed to be working on right now?"

"Science?" said Oak. She had her heavy textbook out on her desk.

"Exactly," said Mr. Rivera. "So—who here knows the meaning of the word *interdisciplinary*? Yes? Marcus?"

"Is that when a student gets in trouble for lots of things at the same time?"

Mr. Rivera laughed, but not in a mean way. "That's a great guess, Marcus, but no. Anyone else? Beck?"

"Doesn't it mean, like, trying to look at a problem from lots of different angles?"

"Exactly, right," said Mr. Rivera, and his smile was so bright and proud of Beck that all the other kids—Alder included—sat up a little straighter, warmed too by that look.

"So, in school, we do math, right? And science and language arts and current events and history."

"And art!" called Cynthia.

"Art!" barked Mr. Rivera, so loud and quick that Alder was a little bit startled. "Yes! Art."

"And PE," said Oak from behind him.

"Indeed," Mr. Rivera said, nodding. "Where would we be without physical education?"

It was a rhetorical question. Alder was mostly sure.

"Okay," said Mr. Rivera. "But even though we think of all those as different subjects, they aren't all that disconnected, really. Things don't fit into neat compartments.

Take, for example . . ." And here he turned around to the whiteboard, scanning the list of words. "Well, take any of them. Arms! Why not? Take *arms*. Which subject, would you say, does *arms* fit into?

"PE?" Miriam said. "Like, push-ups and stuff."

"Yes." Mr. Rivera nodded so vigorously that his hair flopped on his forehead. "But *just* PE?"

The class was quiet for a moment, thinking. Then Oak offered, "Well, weapons are sometimes called *arms*, so I guess, history and current events?"

Mr. Rivera's eyes glistened with excitement. "Perfect," he said. "And, anyone ever heard of an armistice?"

No one answered.

"Look it up!" he said. "Who's got the dictionary?"

No one had the dictionary. It was sitting on a pedestal near the window, closest to Cynthia's desk, so she got up and flipped through the thin pages, tracing her finger down entries until at last she said, "Armistice! Here it is. Noun. It means peace treaty."

"Exactly," said Mr. Rivera. "It means a laying down of arms—of weapons."

"Isn't there a book about war with *arms* in the title?" asked Darla. "My older brother read it last year in high school."

"Indeed," Mr. Rivera said. "*A Farewell to Arms*, by Ernest Hemingway, most likely. So literature too then—so far we have literature, and history, and current events, and physical education."

"The arms of a triangle!" Alder burst out, suddenly and loudly. "Math!"

"Outstanding!" said Mr. Rivera. "Good work, Alder. So what about art? And science?"

"There are lots of paintings of arms," Cynthia offered. "And sculptures."

"Like on the ceiling of the Sistine Chapel," said Miriam. "We went to Italy last summer and saw it, that painting of God and Adam touching fingertips."

"And isn't there a whole part of science all about the human body?" Marcus asked. "What's that called?"

"Physiology," said Mr. Rivera. "Or anatomy. Excellent. So there you go." He circled ARMS an extra time for good measure. "One little word, one part of a person, and look where it has taken us. All through our classroom day, through each subject."

Alder was impressed. The whole time they'd been talking, he'd totally forgotten that they were in school and that Mr. Rivera was giving them an assignment. It had just been fun.

"Okay," said Mr. Rivera, "what I want you all to do is put together an interdisciplinary study of the three words you've circled. For example, let's see . . ." He walked over to Alder and looked at his paper. "So Alder here has circled *toenails*, and *water*, and *family*."

Everyone laughed at *toenails*.

"Who else chose toenails?" Mr. Rivera asked. A bunch of hands went up, more than Alder would have expected. "Okay . . . Marcus!" Mr. Rivera said, pointing. "You're Alder's TOENAIL partner. The two of you can work together to research TOENAILS—figure out a way it connects with each of our classroom subjects and report back."

For a moment, Alder's heart soared.

Then Mr. Rivera continued. "WATER . . . who else picked WATER? Let's see . . . Beck! You can be Alder's WATER partner. And FAMILY? Great! Oak, you and Alder can team up. That's perfect! You two can investigate family *trees*."

Mr. Rivera chuckled at his own joke, but Alder did not join in. Any excitement he'd felt over being paired with Marcus escaped from him like air from a leaky balloon.

"You all get the point now, right? Each of you, find three different people, one for each word you chose."

The class sat quietly, looking at each other, until Mr. Rivera loudly clapped.

"You'll have to get up! Move around! Talk to each other. Let's go!"

And then chairs scraped the linoleum as they were pushed back, and the room filled with the loud chatter of kids yelling back and forth—

"Sebastian, which words did you choose?"

"Did anyone else choose TEETH?"

"I can't *believe* I chose BACTERIA," groaned Cynthia, who had suggested it in the first place. "There aren't any poems about *bacteria*."

In the end, almost everyone found the matches they needed, and then Mr. Rivera helped the few stragglers shift their lists so that no one was left unmatched.

"You see," said Mr. Rivera when they had finally settled back at their desks, a very loud twenty minutes later (during which Alder had had nothing to do, since Mr. Rivera had used him as the example and he was already matched up), "the group of us is like that list of words. We may seem separate and unattached, and maybe some of you don't know each other well yet, but we are connected, we are intertwined. For the next nine months, at least!"

Mr. Rivera probably meant for that to sound uplifting and exciting. But to Alder, looking over his shoulder at Oak and, beyond her, at Beck, it sounded more like a threat than a promise.

At home, however, Fern waited for him. Sleepy, warm, a fuzzy orange puddle on the foot of his bed. She looked up when Alder came into the bedroom, and when he placed his hand on her back, she began to softly purr.

Alder scooped her up and held her against his chest. Her head fit just perfectly under his chin. He sank down onto his bed and leaned back against his pillow.

Fern fell back to sleep, a pleasant floppy weight. But Alder's eyes were open. From where he lay on his bed, he had a good view of his front yard and, now that the walnut tree was just a stump, of Oak's, too. Walking home from the bus stop, he'd felt Oak walking about five paces behind him, but she didn't rush to catch up, and he didn't slow down to wait for her. She'd gone up the driveway to her house without a word to Alder, which he thought had been rather rude, even though he had no desire to speak to her. And by the time he'd gathered Fern and peered out his window, it was to see Oak and *that woman* leaving the house again, climbing into their car and driving away, leaving the construction workers up there on top of the garage, shooting the framework of the new second story with loud nail guns.

There were stacks of construction materials on the neighbors' driveway, boxes and boxes of shingles and rolls of black paper, covered in plastic to protect them. It could be neat to be a construction worker, Alder considered, to use your hands to build something that didn't exist before you started.

But, he thought, his eyes flicking to where the walnut tree used to stand, sometimes building something new meant destroying something old. That Alder didn't like. Not one bit.

Then Alder saw something . . . sort of a flicker, a shimmer, where the old tree had been. It looked to Alder like an extra-shiny patch of air. Probably it was just a reflection off his window, or off one of the windows next door. He stood, Fern still tucked under his chin, and walked toward his window to take a closer look.

It was still there, the shiny spot, hanging in the sky like a window without a frame. And the longer Alder stared at it, the more unsettled he felt.

Alder rubbed Fern's forehead with his thumb. He blinked, and when he looked again for the shiny patch, he couldn't see it anymore.

But though the strange optical illusion had disappeared, Alder's unsettled feeling hadn't.

It was a feeling deep in his gut that something was wrong. Something was torn. Something that was meant to be together wasn't.

Fern awoke and stretched, and one of her tiny, sharp claws ran across Alder's arm, scratching him.

"Ow," he said, but he barely felt the pain from her claw before he forgot it. Because he realized what was wrong. Something was *missing*.

The other kitten. Fern's brother.

"Siblings shouldn't be separated," he said out loud, suddenly, urgently. And he knew it was up to him to set things right.

When Mom got home, Alder was waiting for her on the pink couch. Fern was sharpening her claws on the rug.

"Don't let her do that," Mom said.

Rather than get into a debate about why cats need sharp claws, Alder picked up Fern and set her on the coffee table. Now was not the time to let Mom focus on the downside of pet ownership.

"Mom," he said, "I have something serious we need to talk about."

Alder's mom, who had been unlacing her shoes, looked up. It was sort of funny—her hair falling forward, her shoes half undone, the wide-eyed expression on her face. "What's the matter, Alder?"

"Take your shoes off first," he said. He couldn't have a conversation with her like that.

She kicked them off and joined Alder on the couch. "Is it school?" she asked. "Is it a problem with Marcus?"

Sometimes, his mom was irritatingly perceptive. But none of that was what Alder wanted to talk about. "It's Fern," he said. "I think she misses her brother."

Mom sighed—relieved or annoyed, Alder couldn't tell. "Baby," she said, "Fern is a cat. She's fine."

Alder shook his head. "I don't know," he said, and he picked his words carefully. It felt really important that Mom understood. "It's just . . . Mom, they're siblings. I mean, I don't want you to think I'm ungrateful. I'm really glad you let me get a cat. And it's not that I'm just trying to get a second one! It's just . . . well, earlier, I had this *feeling*.

You know? Like, I knew something suddenly. I knew that it wasn't right to split up siblings. And Mom, if we keep Fern away from her brother, I think I'm going to regret it for the rest of my life."

For a couple of minutes, his mom didn't say anything. She just sat next to Alder, her mouth scrunched up tight. Fern leaped from the coffee table onto the pink velvet couch, landing squarely between them. Absentmindedly, still thinking, Alder's mom ran her hand down the kitten's back.

At last she spoke. "We don't need two cats," she began.

"It's not about *needing* another cat," Alder interrupted, but his mom held up her hand to stop him.

"Let me finish," she said. "We don't need two cats, but I can see that you need this. Okay. We'll go back for Fern's brother."

Alder was so excited that he jumped up and whooped loudly, startling Fern, who puffed up and hissed before jumping off the couch and diving under the coffee table. Then, as if realizing she had overreacted, she stuck out a hind leg and began to casually lick it.

"Come on," Alder said, and he ran to grab his mom's purse.

"Okay," his mom said, going to put her shoes back on, "just don't say that I never did anything for you."

But when they got to the kitten corral at the pet store, only two kittens remained—the black and the tabby. And the girl who'd helped them wasn't there either; in her place was a translucently pale young man, no older than twenty, with a name tag that read "Volunteer" and another that read "Stan," who seemed very interested in something on his phone.

"Excuse me," Alder said, "what happened to the orange kitten?"

"What?" Stan said, not looking up from his phone.

"The orange kitten," Alder said. "Where did he go? Is he in another cage?"

"Oh," said Stan, looking up at last from his phone. "No, that kitten got adopted earlier today."

"That's good news," Alder's mom said, dropping her hand on his shoulder, squeezing it.

It didn't sound like good news to Alder. "Who adopted him?" he asked.

"Sorry, little man," Stan said, smiling. He shoved his phone in the back pocket of his jeans. "We aren't allowed to share that information. How about a different kitten? These are both pretty cute too!"

Alder tried not to cry as he shook his head and turned away. He had failed Fern, and he had failed her brother. They were separated. And now they'd probably never see each other again.

CHAPTER 8

"What will you name him?"

Oak sat cross-legged on the rug in the front room of her new house that felt, suddenly, a lot more like home. In the little diamond of space between her legs, curled into an appealing circle of orange fluff, was the reason why.

"Walnut," Oak answered.

"*Walnut?*" said her mother, who sat nearby. "That's adorable."

Gently, Oak placed her hand on Walnut's fur. Immediately, he began to purr. "I can't believe you let me get a kitten," Oak said. She looked up at her mother and smiled. "Thank you."

"Hey-y," said her mom, smiling back. "That's the first real smile I think I've seen from you since the move."

Oak nodded.

Mom stood up and placed her hand on the top of Oak's head, just as Oak had her hand resting on Walnut's back. "Bedtime soon, okay?"

Oak nodded again and her mom's hand moved away, and Oak heard her footsteps as she headed into the kitchen to finish up the dishes from dinner. Normally, that was Oak's job, and Oak was extra grateful to her mom for taking care of it. She didn't want to disturb the kitten.

But after a minute, he woke up anyway, stretching his two front legs, unsheathing his whisker-thin claws, and yawning, his pink barbed tail uncurling, his needle-sharp tiny teeth gleaming white. He wandered around the room, sniffing the legs of the couch and the bottom row of books. Watching him explore the books, she found it a little bit easier to accept the fact that her mom had undone all her work of arranging the shelves in a rainbow.

When Oak had returned home from school that day, it was to find that the cookbooks were with the cookbooks. The novels were with the novels. And some of the shelves had been repurposed entirely, holding things like picture frames and candles and little decorative carvings. Oak's book rainbow was gone. All her work, disappeared. It had stung, Oak could admit to herself now, with Walnut beside her. Neither Oak nor her mother had mentioned it, but Oak had been angry. Her feelings had been hurt.

She glanced up at the wall clock; it was eight thirty. That meant only five hours had passed since she had gotten off the bus and walked back down Rollingwood Drive to find the construction workers still atop the roof and the shelves rearranged into their mundane categories.

"Let's go run some errands," Mom had said at that moment. Oak had groaned and whined about having just gotten home and needing to do homework, but the truth was that she didn't want to be with her mom right then. She wanted to be alone with her anger about the books. But her mom, it turned out, was in one of those weird moods when she just *insisted* on Oak going with her. After another minute of whining, Oak recognized it was no use, and she'd dumped her backpack just inside the door of her bedroom and reluctantly followed her mom to the car.

First to the gas station.

Then to the grocery store.

Then to the optometrist to pick up Mom's new glasses.

Then back to the grocery store because they had forgotten to get milk.

Then a stop at the drugstore so Mom could pick up a prescription—a boring long line there, but at least Oak noticed the display of DNA test kits near the counter, which gave her an idea for the school project.

And finally, to a coffee shop for fresh-roasted coffee beans because, Mom said, "The first thing to find in a new town is the best place for freshly roasted coffee."

The coffee shop was in a little strip of stores that also included a dry cleaner's, a yoga studio, and a pet store. Mom had gotten her bag of coffee beans and they were walking back to the car when Oak saw the sign on the pet shop's door: CAT ADOPTION FAIR ALL WEEK!

"Mom," she said, and pointed.

Mom read the sign. "Oak, honey," she said, "we've been through this before. We aren't pet people."

"No," said Oak. "That's not what you said. You said we aren't *dog* people. And anyway, I don't see why *you* get to decide what kind of people *we* are."

They were in the middle of the parking lot, and Oak found that she had stopped walking. Mom stopped too, and she rubbed the top of her nose, up close to her eyes, as if Oak was giving her a headache.

"Baby," her mother began, "we've been having such a nice afternoon together. Let's not spoil it, okay?"

A *nice afternoon*? It was as if her mom hadn't even noticed how Oak had been dragging her feet, how she had hardly said a word, how she'd been a totally unwilling participant in this afternoon of boring chores. Just like she hadn't noticed Oak's book spine masterpiece.

Oak could have said all of this. But instead she said, "Mom, you might not be a pet person. But I am. Let's go look at the kittens. Please?"

Mom sighed. She tucked her bag of coffee beans into her purse and said, "Okay, Oak, fine. We can go look at the kittens, if you really want to. But remember, we are *only looking*. Okay?"

Oak grinned, but she didn't say anything. She wasn't making any promises she couldn't keep.

Inside the pet store, off to the right, was a plastic-walled play structure. Oak made a beeline for it, her mother calling after her, "Just looking! Remember!"

Peering into the enclosure, Oak spied two sleeping kittens, a black one and a calico, lumped together. And then she saw a third kitten—orange and white striped—sitting alone, tail curled around its paws, looking, Oak thought, rather lonely.

Mom had caught up to her.

"Mom," Oak said, pointing at the orange kitten. "See?"

"That one's been sort of mopey since last night," said a bored-looking young man, whose name tag read "Stan." He sat on a stool near the enclosure and his thumb flicked up on the screen of his phone.

"How come?" said Oak, crouching down to peer through the clear plastic enclosure at the kitten's face.

"His sister got adopted yesterday," Stan said. "Maybe he misses her."

"I don't think cats miss each other," Mom said.

"Did you ever ask one, ma'am?" Stan said.

This Oak's mom didn't seem to have an answer for, which was very unusual indeed.

Stan stood from his stool and scooped up the kitten with one hand. He offered it to Oak. "Want to hold him?"

Oak did.

"He sure seems to like you," Mom had said at the pet store, squatting down next to Oak. She reached out to stroke the kitten; he was light orange and dark orange stripes all over, with a little white patch just beneath his chin.

"He reminds me of one of those vanilla-orange ice cream bars," Oak said.

"Those used to be my favorite when I was a kid," Mom said.

"Really? I've never seen you eat one."

This Mom didn't answer either. She scratched the kitten's white patch. She stood up. Then she did something that Oak couldn't have expected. She turned to Stan and said, "So, how do we adopt him?"

That was the first time Oak had heard the kitten purr, as soon as her mom had said that. She still couldn't believe, five hours later, watching the kitten exploring their living room, that Mom had changed her mind. And now, here they were—Oak and Walnut—and Oak made a silent promise that she would try not to complain so much—not about the move, not about the bookshelves.

Because even though she missed their place in San Francisco, and even though she missed her friends and her school, if her parents hadn't made her move to Southern California, maybe even if they hadn't moved into this house, she never would have met the kitten—the tiny orange-and-white fluffball of a kitten—who was now her own.

"Oak," Mom called from the kitchen, "let's call your dad before you get ready for bed. You can tell him about the cat!"

"Sure!" Oak stood up. "I'll be there in a minute."

Walnut was trying to jump up onto the window seat in the front window, but he wasn't quite big enough to manage. Oak lifted him up and placed him on the wooden bench. "Just a quick look," Oak told the kitten. "Then let's go say hi to my dad."

The kitten's white whiskers radiated out from his little orange muzzle like sunbeams. His ears twitched forward as he looked through the window, and he lifted one paw and scratched at the glass.

What was he looking at? Oak bent down and angled her head so that she was looking in the same direction as the kitten. Oak couldn't see much, but she'd heard somewhere that cats could see in the dark. Walnut made a funny little sound in his throat—like a meow crossed with a purr—and he scratched at the glass again.

"What is it?" Oak asked. And that's when she saw it: a flicker of movement between her house and the neighbors'. It came and went so quickly that she thought it might have been a hummingbird. No—it couldn't have been a hummingbird . . . they wouldn't be flying around at night. She squinted her eyes a bit and tried to see the movement again.

"Oak," Mom called. "Come say hi to Dad!"

Oak scooped up the kitten and headed to the kitchen. "Wait until you meet my dad," she said to Walnut. "You're going to love him."

Maybe it was the addition of the kitten to the household that put Oak into such a generous mood; whatever the reason, when she headed off to school under a wide, gray sky, thick white clouds way up high, she resolved to make the best of her new situation. So when she heard her neighbor trudging behind her, up the hill toward the bus stop, Oak stopped and waited.

"Hello," she said, and she even smiled.

Alder looked like someone who had not slept the night before—or, if he had slept, it had been fitful and plagued with nightmares. His hair swirled in an unruly mess of curls; his long-sleeved T-shirt was rumpled and half tucked in, as if by accident, and up close, Oak could see hard bits of crust in the inner corners of his eyes. Even worse, Alder didn't respond to her greeting. His hands remained fisted around the straps of his backpack, and after a cursory glance, his gaze returned to the sidewalk. On he went, not breaking his stride, past Oak and toward the corner to meet the bus.

"Rude," Oak mumbled, loud enough to be heard, but ahead of her, Alder didn't flinch.

Never mind him. Oak wasn't going to let her crabby neighbor ruin the first happy morning Oak had had since the move. It was made happier, the morning, by the memory of how she'd left little Walnut—he was curled in a ball near the foot of her bed, his fluffy chest rising and falling with each gentle breath.

Oak channeled the kitten's calm as she focused her eyes on Alder's backpack in front of her. It looked heavy, like he'd brought home all his books the night before. And he walked so *slowly*. There was no reason Oak should have to slow her pace and stay behind him, she decided. After all, she'd done a nice thing by waiting for him and saying hello; if he was too impolite to even answer, then she'd just speed up and push right past him.

And that was what she did. With long, forceful strides, Oak powered up the hill. She caught up to Alder in no time, but even though he had to know that she was wanting to pass, he stayed stubbornly in the middle of the sidewalk.

"Rude," Oak said again, and then she stepped up next

to Alder's right side, shoving a little with her left elbow to make room.

She didn't push *that* hard, but maybe she did push harder than she'd intended. Or maybe Alder's backpack had been even heavier than it looked. But whatever the reason, when Oak's elbow pushed into Alder's side, it knocked him off-balance, and the next thing Oak knew, he was down on the sidewalk, arms flailing, a surprised "Oof!" coming out of his mouth.

Maybe she should have stopped to help him up.

Probably she should have.

But, Oak thought, probably *he* should have answered when she had said hello.

And so, with a bright flame of meanness springing to life in her chest, Oak stomped on up the hill, cresting it just as the yellow-orange school bus rounded the corner and pulled to a stop.

The door hissed open, and Oak mounted the steps.

"Hello, tree girl," said Faith with a smile.

"Hey," Oak answered, and she headed up the aisle.

"What's up, tree boy?" Oak heard Faith say behind her. And then, "Alder, buddy, what happened to your hands?"

"It's nothing," Oak heard Alder mumble. "I just scraped them."

"You need a Band-Aid," Faith said, and the concern in her voice made Oak's breakfast curdle in her stomach. Oak hadn't noticed that Alder had gotten hurt.

"I'll be okay," Alder said.

Oak tucked herself into an empty row, parking her backpack on her lap.

She looked out the window and pretended not to see Alder as he walked by, pretended not to see the red scrapes on his palms, pretended not to notice the way he stopped and looked around for a seat before he disappeared into a back row.

Outside, the clouds gathered and darkened. As the bus's door closed with another hiss and the bus pulled onto the street with a screech, Oak heard a third sound—a rumble of thunder, far away.

CHAPTER 9

When the bus's doors opened in front of the school and the kids climbed down the steps, it was into a light drizzle of rain. Alder's hands, scraped raw, still stung, and he held them flat in front of himself to let the cold water mist them. It felt better.

"Wow, that looks pretty bad." It was Beck. "Maybe you should go to the nurse's office before class. Do you want me to go with you?"

Alder, who had fully intended to go to the nurse's office, said, "It's fine," and shrugged as if the scrapes were no big deal.

"You should get, like, an antiseptic spray or something," suggested Marcus, who was next to Beck.

"It's no big deal, all right?" Alder didn't mean to raise his voice, and as soon as the words were out, he was embarrassed by how loud they'd been. He tried again. "I'll be fine," he said.

"Whatever," Marcus said, and he and Beck went into the school building.

A fat droplet landed in the palm of Alder's outstretched hand. The rain was coming down heavier now, and he hurried up the steps toward the entrance.

"Hey," said a voice behind him—Oak's. "I'm sorry you got hurt."

"Sure you are," said Alder, and he wasn't even sure what he meant by that.

"I *am* sorry," Oak said again. She pulled open the door and held it for him to pass through.

Alder didn't say anything. He headed for the bathroom to rinse off his hands.

When he got to class a few minutes later, everyone else was already in their seats. He'd washed his hands and patted the scrapes dry with a paper towel. It wasn't much, but it was better. He slumped out of his backpack and slid into his seat, looking through the window at the falling rain. It was coming down harder now. Maybe it would be a real storm.

He hoped so. He hoped it rained and rained and rained.

Sometimes, wishes come true. It did rain and rain and rain, all morning long; it rained so much that the class had to eat lunch inside, at their desks. After they finished eating, Mr. Rivera facilitated a game of Heads Up, Seven Up, and even though Alder screwed tight his eyes and held his thumb straight up, no one picked him, not once in the game's three rounds.

Oak, Alder noticed, got picked every single time.

And then, after lunch, Mr. Rivera said it was time for them to get with their partners to work on their Pieces of a Person project.

"We're going to spend fifteen minutes with each partner, for a total of forty-five minutes," Mr. Rivera said. "I've worked out a spreadsheet of who's with who for what." He waved a piece of paper in the air, and Alder could see that Mr. Rivera had color-coded the list.

"First pairings," Mr. Rivera said, and he began to read a list of names. Alder tuned him out until he heard his own name: "Alder, you and Marcus are together for TOE-NAILS."

Alder perked up. Maybe this would be good—a chance for him and Marcus to sit together for a few minutes, just the two of them. Maybe they would have a really good time and Marcus would remember why they were best friends, and he'd say something like *I don't know why we haven't been hanging out together! Want to come over to my place after school?*

Feeling cautiously optimistic, Alder gathered up the

research about toenails he'd done the night before and scooted his chair next to Marcus's desk, trying not to show that he cared that Marcus hadn't moved *his* chair to Alder's desk.

"Hey, Marcus," Alder said, immediately hating how eager his voice sounded.

"Hey," Marcus said, his voice sounding bored.

"So, uh, toenails," said Alder, feeling like a complete idiot.

"Yeah," said Marcus. "I don't know why I wrote that down. I wish I would have chosen something else. Anything else."

"Yeah," said Alder, though he had been sort of excited about all the weird information he'd found about toenails. "Me too."

Marcus sighed heavily. "Well," he said, "let's get this over with."

Marcus's heavy sigh punctured Alder's excitement; he felt the air going out of him, like a deflating balloon. Defeatedly, Alder pulled out his research and scanned the list of facts he'd compiled. "Um," he said, "well, toenails are made of the same stuff—keratin, a protein—as animal hooves and horns."

Marcus nodded and wrote that down.

"And," said Alder, "toenails are basically human claws."

"That's sort of cool, I guess," said Marcus. "And I read

that toenails are, like, basically full of bacteria, all the time. Like, underneath."

Alder nodded and wrote that down, even though he'd discovered the same research already. Then he said, "Do you know about the world's longest toenails?"

"No," said Marcus. "Gross!"

"Yeah," said Alder. "They belong to a woman who lives not too far from here. In Compton. They're, like, six inches long."

"How does she wear shoes?"

"That's the thing," Alder said, and Marcus's eyes widened at the fact that Alder had more information. This was more like it. "She only wears flip-flops! If she lived somewhere that got really cold, where she had to, like, wear snow boots or something, she couldn't have grown them so long."

"Huh," said Marcus, and he looked out the window where the rain was coming down in sheets. "What do you think she's doing right now?"

That was an excellent question. Alder stared into the rain, too, and imagined the woman with the world's longest toenails, splashing in her flip-flops through rising puddles. "She's out there somewhere, doing something," he said, more to himself than to Marcus, but Marcus nodded, like he knew exactly what Alder meant and how Alder felt . . . sort of amazed to think that the woman with the world's longest toenails was a *person*, a real, living, breathing, walking person who might be caught out in the rain, right at that very moment, and just down the road.

A moment passed, Marcus and Alder together, wondering. Then Marcus said, "Hey, maybe, like, for extra credit, we could do a comic strip about the world's-longest-toenail lady in the rain. You can do the pictures and I'll write the words."

"Okay," Alder said. It was a really good idea, but Alder was so glad to feel like a team again with Marcus that he probably would have agreed to pretty much anything Marcus had suggested in that moment.

They spent a happy ten minutes together, thinking about their toenail comic strip, until Mr. Rivera called, "Time to switch groups!"

The warm, happy feeling of having been close to Marcus buoyed Alder as he drifted from Marcus's desk to Oak's, where he positioned his chair and sat back down.

"Hey," Oak said. "I'm sorry again about what happened to your hands."

Alder barked a laugh. "What *happened* to my hands?"

Oak blushed, but she looked mad. "I don't know what more you want me to say," she said.

Alder wanted to tell her that there was a big difference between saying she was sorry for "what happened" to his hands and being sorry that she shoved him. Saying she was sorry for what happened didn't really *mean* anything. It was like him falling down had nothing to do with Oak. Like it was something that *just happened* instead of something that she *made* happen.

But instead of saying any of that, Alder just said, "Whatever." He felt his good mood melting away.

"So," Oak said, in a tone that made it clear that she thought the whole incident was behind them, "how do you want to do this family project?"

Alder shrugged. "Whatever," he said again.

Oak raised an eyebrow. "Well, I have an idea for the science section. What if we both did one of those kits? You know, where you send in a DNA sample and they tell you about your family? We could record the results for our project. I'll bet no one else is doing that."

"How do they work?" Alder asked. It was, he thought begrudgingly, a good idea.

"It's pretty simple. You can buy the tests at the drugstore—I just saw them when I was running errands with my mom. You fill a little plastic vial with spit—"

"Gross," said Alder.

Oak shrugged. "Sometimes science is gross. *Anyway,* then you mail it to the company and they analyze your DNA from the spit sample. Then they send you information about who your ancestors are, and what part of the world they were from."

"Is it expensive?"

"Sort of," said Oak. "The one I saw costs fifty-nine dollars."

"I have some money saved up," said Alder. "From birthdays."

"I've got almost a hundred dollars from the yard sale we had before we moved," said Oak.

"It could be kind of cool," Alder admitted.

"So, do you want to do it?"

Alder shrugged. "Whatever," he said, for the third time.

Oak pressed her lips together into a thin, angry line. Then she said, "If you're going to be like that, then we can just sit here and each work on the other sections separately. I don't care either way."

"Whatever," Alder said again, and this time, the word felt satisfying.

When the school day was over and they went outside to meet the bus, it was to a lightning-cracked sky.

It was only just past three o'clock, but already the sky looked evening-dark. Wind blew, strong and cold, battering raindrops hard like pellets into Alder's face, which he tucked into the collar of his jacket as he hurried onto the bus.

Faith's cheeks were flushed a cheerful red; she had the bus's heater cranked up, and it was a welcome rush of warmth after the cold wet wind outside.

"It's a real storm," she said with a smile, like this was great news.

Once the bus was loaded, Faith pulled a little knob next to the steering wheel to turn on the headlights; they cut a bright hole into the darkening day. "Here we go," she said, and they were off.

Rain pounded down onto the bus's metal roof, sounding like someone was throwing handfuls of pebbles down at them. They stayed in the far-right lane, and in places where the gutters were overfull, the bus's wheels splashed waves up onto the sidewalk. Each time this happened, the busful of children cheered. Every few minutes, lightning lit the sky as brightly as the flash of a camera; then, in unison, the kids counted, "One, two, three, four . . . ," until the thunder struck, like an answer to the lightning's call.

The bus had the raucous atmosphere of a party and the musty scent of damp hair and clothes.

By the time they reached the hill at the top of Rollingwood Drive, rain was coming down so fiercely that Faith called over her shoulder, "Tree kids! I'll take the bus down the street and drop you at your houses. What are your addresses?"

"Fifteen!" called Alder, relieved to not have to walk down the street in the rain.

"Eleven," called Oak.

Faith cranked the enormous steering wheel and maneuvered down Rollingwood Drive, pulling to a stop between their houses. "That's funny," she said as Alder made his way to the front of the bus. "There's no Thirteen."

Alder blinked. Faith was right—his house was number Fifteen, and right next door was Oak's house, number Eleven. How had he never noticed that before?

"Maybe they thought it was bad luck to number a house Thirteen," Faith said.

Lightning flashed, and in the sudden bright light, everything in the bus looked . . . a little strange. Alder shivered, though he wasn't cold. The bus filled with the voices of the other kids, counting, waiting for the thunder to follow.

"One, two, three . . ."

This time, when the thunder struck, it was with a terrible *crack*, like the world was splitting. Behind him, a hand grabbed Alder's arm.

"Sorry," Oak said. "That was scary."

"All right, tree kids," Faith said. "See you tomorrow."

She pulled the lever to open the bus's door, and Alder and Oak went out into the storm. The harsh wind pressed them together for one moment, and then each took off, Alder up his driveway and Oak up hers, trying, separately but together, to outrun the storm.

CHAPTER 10

Oak's mom wouldn't be home from the office for another hour or so. And because of the rain, the construction workers weren't on the roof either. Oak unlocked the front door and slammed inside, breathing heavily from the run and dripping onto the entry hall floor. She let her backpack slide to the entry hall rug, and she pulled down the zipper on her sweatshirt. It was heavy with rainwater, soaked nearly through, just from the time it had taken her to go from the bus to her front door.

It felt good to be safe and sound inside. Oak knelt to untie her shoes, and at the same time she called, "Walnut! Here, kitty!"

There was no answer. Oak stayed still, hands on the laces of her sneaker, and listened.

Nothing.

"Walnut?" she called again.

When there was still no sound—no meow, no thump from the kitten jumping off the bed—Oak stood up, shoes still tied. Slowly, she walked through the living room and toward the hallway to her bedroom.

A terrible feeling was beginning to rise in her, a feeling she couldn't connect to anything particular—just the uncomfortable, anxious knowledge that in a moment she would realize something.

The door to her bedroom was partway closed. Maybe that was why Walnut hadn't heard her calling him, Oak thought, but she knew that wasn't true. She knew she was lying to herself. Slowly, Oak pushed open the door. She stepped into her room.

Oh, it was cold! Wind leaked in like a ghost through the window that—oh, no—the window that Oak had left cracked open that morning before school, thinking that a little fresh air would be good for Walnut.

But now, Oak saw, the screen had come loose—was it from the wind? The rain? She didn't know, only that it *was* loose, and the window was open, and Walnut was gone.

"No," she whispered, and she spun around and ran for the front door. "Walnut," she called, throwing open the door.

The storm had redoubled. The sky, a flat plane of steel

gray, felt oppressively close, and rain flew in sideways sheets, soaking through Oak's long-sleeved T-shirt in seconds. "Walnut!" she called again. Her hair dripped in strings across her face, and she wiped it back.

What was that—there, by the tree stump, did she see something? A flash, a movement, maybe something orange? It was there—she was sure of it! But then Oak blinked the rain from her eyes and it was gone.

Maybe it was her kitten. Oak headed toward the tree stump, leaning into the wind. "Walnut!" she called, and then she heard something—

Another voice, sounding as desperate as she felt, yelling, "Fern!"

She didn't have time to wonder what that was about. Her kitten was out here somewhere, alone, soaking wet, scared. And it was *her* fault.

"Walnut!" she called again, pushing into the wind—it was almost as if the wind's hands were on her shoulders, trying to push her back, but she leaned even farther forward, she *insisted* her way toward the tree stump, where she had seen the flash of orange.

Nearer now, the other voice called, "Fern!"

And then it was nearly upon her—"Fern!" There was Alder, under the large canopy of a black umbrella, pushing forward, as she was, to the same spot in the yard. The wind cruelly pressed on the umbrella's fabric, folding it inward.

Alder was using it like a shield, holding it in front of himself as he pushed forward, and Oak could tell that he didn't see her there in front of him.

"Hey!" she called before he could jab her with the umbrella's sharp spike. He stopped abruptly, and his sudden shift allowed the wind to catch underneath the umbrella's canopy, flipping it inside out to reveal its silver skeleton beneath.

It would have been funny except that just then, three things happened: first, both Oak and Alder saw the same dash of orange movement—"My kitten!" they both called. Second, Oak remembered with an icy shock of fear that one should never carry anything metal during a storm, and she moved to knock the umbrella from Alder's hand. And third, a ragged flash of lighting tore across the sky.

And then, there was nothing.

CHAPTER 11

When Alder opened his eyes, it was to find that he and Oak were no longer outside in the rain. They were inside, somewhere, and staring at a front door.

It wasn't Alder's front door; it wasn't Oak's, either. But it could have been, almost. This door had the same three skinny rectangular panes of glass set along the top of the door, just as did Oak's, just as did Alder's. The knob was a silver orb, just like Oak's, just like Alder's. But unlike Oak's front door, which was painted orange, and unlike Alder's door, which was painted green, this door was not painted at all. Natural wood grains swirled across its surface in burls and whirls and knots. And they seemed almost to shimmer.

Alder looked away from the door and over at Oak, who turned to him with eyes round as records.

"Are we in your house?" Alder whispered.

Oak shook her head. "Are we in yours?"

Alder didn't bother pointing out that if they had been in his house, he wouldn't have asked Oak if they were in *hers*. He just shook his head.

Then he heard a sound—a movement—coming from behind them.

Alder turned to see that the house in which they found themselves was laid out identically to his—a short entry hall that branched, to the left, into a smallish family room and led, to the right, to another hallway which, he assumed, would lead to three small bedrooms. The sound had come from the left—the family room.

Lightning lit up the hallway for a quick second, like the flash of a camera, and then came an ominous rumble of thunder.

Alder and Oak looked at one another. Without a word, they turned back to the door, reaching in unison for the knob, anxious to get out of . . . wherever they were. But before they reached it, they heard another sound that froze them in their tracks.

Meow.

"Fern," said Alder.

"Walnut," said Oak.

And they turned together back down the hallway, leaving the door behind them.

In the living room, the only light came from the fireplace, cheerfully crackling. Orange flames licked the logs, and just as Oak and Alder crossed the threshold, a log popped and sent a spark zigzagging upward into the chimney.

There was a shelf crowded full of odd little knickknacks, a table set for tea, a fringed antique rug with a fading, complicated pattern of vines and flowers. A low-backed couch and an overstuffed chair, angled toward the fireplace.

Someone was sitting in the chair; Oak and Alder could only see the top of the person's head, the messy tuft of brownish-grayish hair.

Whoever sat in the chair was no taller than a child. Oak and Alder could see legs, too short to reach the floor, and swinging feet, wearing shining brown leather boots.

Then, they heard it again—*Meow*.

Emboldened, Alder stepped forward.

Beside him, Oak cleared her throat and said, "Excuse me. I wonder—is that my kitten?"

"*Your* kitten?" Alder nearly forgot for the moment that they were in a stranger's house, that they had no idea how they had gotten there. "If it's anyone's kitten, it's *my* kitten."

"There, there, children." came a voice from the chair. It was a male voice, but rather high-pitched, and it was not a voice either Alder or Oak had ever heard before. "No need to argue," the voice continued, and then the feet stretched toward the floor, and the owner of the feet and the voice plopped out of the chair. "We'll sort everything out," he said. "After all, there is more than one way to skin a cat."

A noise came out of Alder—kind of a squeak—and beside him, Oak cleared her throat uncomfortably.

And then the odd little figure stepped away from the chair and toward Alder and Oak, who still stood in the room's open doorway. As he scuttled toward them, Alder reached out and clutched Oak's arm. She put her hand on top of his.

The boots caught and reflected the flames as if they'd recently been shined. Above the boots were woolen socks—tall ones—and then short pants—not shorts, exactly, for they fell below the knee and had buttons there, cinching them close. Above the short pants was a waistcoat and a watch chain that disappeared into a small pocket, presumably where a watch was resting.

And there was an orange kitten cradled in two hands—strange, tiny, pink hands—and then there was the face. Hair all over, white in the center, fading out to grayish brown, and a long, pointed snout, with a burst of bristly white whiskers on either side. Jewel-black eyes—shiny—and when the creature smiled, two uneven rows of pointed ivory teeth grinned out.

Alder felt his mouth flopping open and shut like a fish's.

"Hello," said the creature. "I'm Mort. I've been waiting for you."

It *couldn't* be Mort, thought Alder.

Except, of course, it was—Mort, the taxidermied opossum from his bookshelf at home, but now here, the size of a six-year-old child, fully dressed, and clutching, Alder was certain, his kitten, Fern.

That was the most important part of this situation, he decided with a clarity that surprised him. He had to get Fern safely away, and then, later, he could try to work out what exactly all of this meant.

But then Oak stepped forward. "Walnut!" she said. "You have my kitten—what are you doing to my kitten?"

"*Your* kitten?" said Alder. "That's Fern!"

"I don't know who Fern is," said Oak, and she stomped her foot, sounding angry. "All I know is that . . . *thing* has my Walnut. Give him back. At once!"

Mort began to hop a little, foot to foot, nervously. "Well, well," he said, and his boots made clippity-cloppity sounds on the wood floor, like a pony might. "Well, well." He seemed, Alder thought, as if *he* were a little bit afraid of *them*.

And then the creature backed up to set the kitten down on the chair—gently, Alder noticed—before suddenly, freakishly, curling his black-tinged lips back into an awful grin and freezing in place, his eyes shining like marbles.

Meow, said the kitten, and it hopped down from the chair and began sniffing the boots of the completely unmoving opossum.

"What is happening?" Oak asked. She was trembling all over; her hands were shaking, her teeth chattering. It was fear.

"I think . . . ," said Alder, and he stepped slowly forward, toward the frozen figure, "I think . . . he's playing possum."

It was impossible that this figure was actually Mort, the harmless taxidermied opossum that had stood, all of Alder's life, on the bookshelf in the front room of his home. But, impossible or not, it seemed that, indeed, this Mort was somehow a version of his very own Mort.

And perhaps it was because of his lifetime affection for the smaller Mort, or perhaps it was because his father had given Mort to his mother as a gift many years ago . . . whatever the reason, Alder found that he did not feel afraid anymore, but rather almost overwhelmed by a desire to help this creature who, he was certain, needed him.

"It's okay," Alder said, taking slow and careful steps away from the doorway and toward the dummy-still Mort. "We aren't going to hurt you," he soothed, and his voice was gentle like his mother's sometimes was, the voice he used with his kitten back at home.

The kitten—Alder's eyes flitted away from Mort and down to the orange cat still sniffing the polished boots. It did look quite a bit like his Fern, but, Alder realized, this kitten was bigger than Fern, rounder of belly and wider of face.

"Walnut," said Oak behind him, and the kitten turned and pranced, purred and wound himself between Oak's legs until she scooped him up.

Fern was still missing, and whether she was here or back in his yard or someplace else entirely, Alder did not know. He would find her, Alder promised, but first, he had to help Mort.

"It's okay," said Alder again, and he reached out a hand, hesitating a moment before resting it gently on the opossum's wrist, which stuck out past the sleeve of his jacket, the fur there looking so vulnerably exposed. The fur was soft, just like Mort's fur back home, but there was warmth underneath—the pulse of life. Alder could feel the rapid fluttering of Mort's pulse just beneath his pelt.

Then there was another noise—*Mew*—and this time it *was* Alder's kitten who emerged, as if nothing was unusual at all, from Mort's kitchen.

Alder bent to pick up Fern, and he held her soft, warm body close to his chest and kissed her sweet little head. She began to purr, a loud and friendly rumble that seemed much too large for her body.

"Ah," said Mort, whose arms dropped to his sides. He shook his head as if to clear it. "Sorry about that. Old habits die hard."

CHAPTER 12

Mort offered to heat up some cider, but both Alder and Oak refused politely.

"Cider gives me a stomachache," said Oak. In truth, she was simply a bit nervous about accepting a hot drink from a four-foot opossum she'd only just met, but Mort looked so saddened by her pronouncement that Oak felt immediately sorry for having lied. Which was such a weird way to feel—sorry? In a situation like this? Where the whole world seemed to be make-believe—like a dream or a hallucination?

Maybe she *was* hallucinating, Oak thought. Maybe she was in a coma or something, because of the lightning.

But until she figured out what was going on, or until she woke up, she might as well see how this played out.

So, when the weird opossum creature gestured for her to take a seat, Oak slid into a spot on the low-backed couch, her kitten sleeping like a warm little nut on her lap. She was glad when Alder sat next to her, so close that their legs nearly touched. In *his* lap was a kitten who looked so much like Walnut that there was only one explanation. This, at least, was a thing that she could make sense of.

"We adopted siblings," she said. "You named yours Fern?"

Alder nodded. "I named her after our plant. Yours is Walnut?"

"I named her after the tree," said Oak, and Alder nodded again. Oak didn't have to explain which tree she meant.

"That's pretty weird," said Alder, but, Oak thought, compared to the company in which they currently found themselves, the kitten coincidence was not nearly as strange as it otherwise might have seemed.

Mort had moved his chair so that its back was to the fire, and he'd added another log so that the fire crackled merrily, and then he hopped up into his seat, scooting his rump comfortably back, settling himself into place as if he'd done it a thousand times. "Now," he said with a smile, and Oak really wished that his teeth weren't quite so sharp, "Alder, why don't you do the introductions?"

Alder *knew* this thing? Oak hadn't thought she could be any more surprised, but here she was.

"Wait," she began, "you . . . know each other?"

Alder cleared his throat. "Well," he said, "in a way. Um, Mort, you've already met Fern and Walnut, I guess, and this is Oak. She's my new neighbor. They just moved in next door. Oak, this is . . . Mort."

"I'm pleased to make your acquaintance," said Mort, and his voice was stiffly formal, as if he were happy to have a chance to break out his fancy vocabulary.

"Likewise," said Oak, though she wasn't exactly *pleased* to make his acquaintance. Still, she had manners, and her mom would probably be proud that she remembered them, even in this bizarre situation. Politely, Oak asked, "So, where exactly are we?"

"On a couch, in my front room," said Mort. Oak wished that his smile wasn't so terrifying.

"But . . . *where* is your couch? *Where* is your front room?" asked Alder.

Now Oak was even more confused. Alder knew this creature, but he didn't know where they were? She was starting to get a headache from all her questions.

"Ah," said Mort, and Oak leaned forward. Mort seemed like he was getting ready to explain everything, which would be such a relief. But before he said another word, his attention was taken by something he seemed to see outside, for he hopped down from his chair and scurried over to the front window to peer outside. "The storm is almost over," he mused. He turned back to face them. His whiskers bristled forward, vibrating. "Children," he said, "you've recovered your kittens, and it's time for you to go."

And he gestured with his tiny pink hands for them to get up, which they did, and he ushered them to the front door.

Oak protested, "But—"

"It's been lovely," Mort interrupted, reaching for the silver doorknob and turning it.

"Thank you for the hospitality," said Alder.

He sounded relieved to be leaving, but Oak wasn't in quite such a hurry to be rushed off. She had questions. Lots of them.

"Wait a minute," she said, but Mort the opossum scooted them both out of his house, onto the front porch. And then he made a formal little bow, so stiff and old-fashioned that it would have been funny if the whole thing hadn't been so impossible.

"Goodbye," said Mort. He shut the door firmly, and Oak heard it click into place, and then he was gone.

CHAPTER 13

One moment, they were being ushered out an open door; the next, Alder heard the click of the door closing.

But when he turned to look over his shoulder, there was no door.

There was no house.

Alder was standing on the stump where the tree had once been; Fern was curled in his arms, and beside him, Oak cradled Walnut and looked around, her expression as bewildered as Alder felt.

The storm had passed. Silver-gray clouds populated the sky, but they did not menace or threaten; they drifted apart, like guests at the end of a party. The air felt damp and electric. There across the lawn, pushed up against the flower bed beneath his front room window, was the broken, twisted shape of his umbrella.

Alder shivered.

"I've got to go," said Oak, and she stumbled away from him toward her house.

"Wait!" Alder called after her, but Oak shook her head and didn't turn back. He watched as she pushed open her front door and disappeared inside.

In his arms, Fern stretched her legs and squirmed as though she wanted down.

"Oh no, you don't," Alder said, and he headed back toward home with one last look behind him, at where the house had been.

Inside, things were so normal that it seemed impossible that he could have just experienced what he had indeed experienced.

Alder closed his front door and kicked off his shoes. Fern tucked under his arm, he went into his bedroom, where he found a puddle under the window and the screen knocked loose from its attachment. Setting Fern on the bed, Alder rehooked the screen and then shut the window firmly. Fern settled onto his pillow and began nonchalantly cleaning her tail, as if nothing peculiar had happened at all.

He was soaking wet, Alder realized suddenly, and very cold. He needed to get out of his wet clothes, but first there was something he had to check. He padded in his socks to the front room and over to the bookcase. There, just as he should be, was Mort—on all fours, opossum size, attached to his wooden base.

When he heard the doorknob twist behind him, Alder whirled around, preparing to see the other Mort burst into his house. But it was just Mom, arms full of grocery bags. She shut the door and shook her head like a wet dog, spraying water droplets.

"Looks like the storm got you, too," she said to Alder, smiling. "That was a big one, wasn't it?"

Alder opened his mouth, but nothing came out. How could he possibly explain what he had just experienced? As the minutes ticked by, he was rapidly beginning to doubt that any of it—the strange house, the crackling fireplace, the oversize Mort—had actually happened at all.

"You look soaked to the skin," Mom said. She kicked off her shoes and made her way to the kitchen, putting the grocery bags on the counter. "Why don't you go take a nice hot bath, and I'll get dinner started."

Alder didn't answer. He just nodded and headed toward the bathroom. A bath. That sounded nice.

Alder filled the bathtub with water as hot as he could stand. He had to climb in slowly, inch by inch, acclimating himself to the warmth. At last, he sighed and immersed himself, dipping even his head into the water, and his ears, just his face above the surface.

It was quiet like that, and peaceful—him floating, loose-limbed, ears plugged by water. It felt safe.

And Alder found that he didn't quite want to think about what had happened, or hadn't happened, where he might have been, or where he might not have been. It was much more likely, he was coming to believe, that none of it had happened at all. That he had simply experienced a hallucination, or maybe just a dream.

There had been a storm, and lightning, and, after all, he'd been carrying a metal-framed umbrella.

"Stupid, stupid," Alder chastised himself, though with his ears underwater, his voice sounded muted and far away.

Maybe a bolt of lightning had struck the umbrella, and the shock of it had knocked him unconscious, and for some reason his brain had conjured up the whole thing, like some weird fever dream. That made a whole lot more sense than an oversize, fully clothed, walking, talking Mort inhabiting a mysterious house that appeared and disappeared.

And, Alder decided, feeling better by the minute, there was no sense in worrying his mom with all of this. After all, if he told her that he'd been struck by lightning, she'd want to take him to the doctor—probably even to the emergency room—and who could tell what they would want to do there? Tests of some kind.

Alder couldn't imagine what kind of tests they might run at the hospital, but he suspected that needles might be involved, and the drawing of blood, which Alder hated more than almost anything. At his eleven-year-old wellness check, he had been surprised, and not in a good way, by what his pediatrician cheerfully called a "screening," which sounded like they were going to see a movie but instead involved the withdrawal of three small vials of his blood, extracted from the inside of his elbow by a needle and a long clear tube. He was in no great hurry to go through *that* again.

And besides, Alder told himself as he flipped the stopper to drain the tub, listening from beneath the waterline as the bath began to empty, he was perfectly fine. Whatever might have happened was behind him. What mattered was that he was safe, and Fern was safe, and the storm was over.

With that resolved, and feeling much better now, Alder dried off and put on his softest pajamas, along with thick warm socks. And then he went to join his mother for dinner.

When he woke the next morning, the sky outside his window was the brightest, clearest blue Alder had ever seen. It was becoming increasingly difficult to believe that a storm had even happened, let alone the strange, impossible oddities that were so ridiculous as to almost make Alder laugh.

Still, he double-checked all the doors and windows before he headed off to the bus stop—no reason to tempt fate, he told himself, picking up Fern for a moment and kissing her fuzzy head to say goodbye.

But when he saw that Oak was standing in the space between their two driveways, as if she were waiting for someone, he felt his stomach begin to curdle. Alder had no desire to discuss what might or might not have happened. It became evident quite quickly, however, that the conversation was going to take place with or without him.

"I've been waiting out here for nearly twenty minutes," Oak said, but her tone was cheerful. "Did you sleep at all last night? I barely did. I was tossing and turning until three o'clock in the morning!"

Alder grunted, vaguely.

Oak must have taken the sound as encouragement, for she went on, "I've been trying to figure out what on earth *happened* to us. That was the weirdest thing that I have ever experienced in my life. And that . . . *thing* . . . you *know* him?"

She was talking about Mort, Alder knew, which meant that his theory about electrocution must have been wrong, if Oak had the same memory. "He's not a *thing*," Alder said, speeding up a little as they headed to the bus stop, as if he could somehow escape Oak and all her energy, all her questions. "He's an opossum."

"A four-foot-tall, talking opossum who wears boots and carries a pocket watch," Oak said, too loudly, Alder thought.

"Shh," he said crossly, though he didn't know why it felt important that no one hear them.

"How do you *know* him?" Oak pressed.

They had reached the corner. And here came the bus. Alder didn't want to talk about any of this, but he *definitely* didn't want to talk about it on the bus. "Later," he said as the bus pulled to a stop, as the doors hissed open.

"When?" said Oak, her voice insistent.

"*Later,*" Alder said again. He began to climb the steps and looked over his shoulder at Oak.

Her lips were pressed together in a line; her hands, on the straps of her backpack, were tight fists. It was obvious that he wasn't getting out of this. "Come over after school," he said begrudgingly. "I'll show you."

All day long, Alder kept an eye on Oak wherever he could: in Mr. Rivera's class; at recess and at lunch; during PE, when they had to run around the track. Oak, he noticed, was surrounded by a circle of friends wherever she went, even though she was so new to the school.

It seemed, he felt, terribly unfair. He felt this especially keenly during PE, at the end of the day, when he noted that not only was Oak surrounded by a circle of friends, she also seemed to have no trouble at all taking off from the pack when she was ready to run—swifter than them all, like she was made for it.

"You should join the cross-country club," Marcus yelled admiringly as she flew by him and Beck, who were taking turns timing each other doing sprints.

"Maybe," Oak called back.

Marcus had never asked *him* if he wanted to join the cross-country club, Alder thought miserably, clutching a cramp at his side as he jogged slowly around the track. Not that he would have wanted to. But it would have been nice to be asked.

Finished with their sprints, Beck and Marcus loped onto the track. Alder watched the way they matched each other, pace for pace, Marcus lengthening his strides to keep up with Beck's longer legs. They were laughing about something.

Were they laughing at *him*? Alder quickened his pace, tried to stand up straighter, to look more athletic.

Beck and Marcus had disappeared from Alder's sight line; they were so much faster than he was that they'd rounded the bend and would be coming up behind him soon. He imagined what he looked like from behind: his T-shirt was sticking to his back, sweaty, and he knew his hair got fluffy and unruly when he ran. He probably looked ridiculous.

Here they came.

"Looking good, Alder," called Beck as they flew by, bread-and-buttering around him.

"Thanks," Alder called back, trying not to sound as winded as he was, but then immediately doubting his response—had Beck been sincere? Was he being mean?

Exhausted both by running and the mental effort of

trying to decide what everything *meant*, Alder slowed to a walk, then stopped, hands on his knees as he tried to catch his breath. The cramp in his side had tightened to a sharp pain. He closed his eyes against the brightness of the sun.

At the end of the day, just like usual, Faith was waiting for them in the bus.

"Hiya, Alder, welcome aboard," she said.

"Hiya, Faith," Alder answered, but his heart just wasn't in it.

At the top of Rollingwood Drive, Faith said, "See ya, tree kids," as Alder followed Oak down the three black stairs. And then the bus pulled away.

Alder trudged down the hill toward home. Oak was at his side. He could feel her there, the way she rolled up onto her toes with each step.

"I'll just pop home and drop off my stuff," Oak said. "Then I'll come over."

At least Mom wasn't home, Alder thought. Her car was gone, and a note on the kitchen counter told him that she'd be gone for a while:

> *Off to the bank and the post office and the library!*
> *Clean that stinky litter box.*
> *xoxo*
> *Mom*

When she went to the library, Alder's mom could lose track of time entirely. Once she'd sat right down in an aisle, so taken by a book's description, and had read the whole thing then and there, cover to cover.

Meow, said Fern. She hopped down from her cushion in the patch of sunlight on the window bench and stretched, front legs sticking straight out, her rump and tail way up in the air behind her.

Alder took a minute to scratch her head, and then he got the scooper and a paper bag. The litter box, which they kept in the smaller bathroom, *did* smell a bit suspicious.

He'd managed to clean it, scrub his hands, and spray some air freshener in the litter box's general direction before he heard Oak knocking at his door.

"Coming," he called, and he picked up Fern before he opened the door so that she couldn't dart outside.

There was Oak, and she'd brought someone—Walnut.

"Hi," said Oak. "I thought I'd bring Walnut over to see Fern. You know, since they're related. I don't know . . . it just doesn't seem right to keep siblings apart."

Alder relaxed a bit for the first time in what felt like forever. Maybe Oak noticed it, because she smiled. Alder smiled back. He opened the door wider. "Great idea," he said.

CHAPTER 14

It was the second house in two days that Oak had been inside that looked both the same as her house and also totally different. The *shape* was the same—the short entry hall; the living room off to the left and the hallway, presumably with bedrooms, off to the right; the wooden window seat in the living room. The pass-through to the kitchen and the dining room. But everything else was different. Oak's house had been covered in a coat of white paint right before they moved in—all the walls, all the ceilings the same bright noncolor. "Fresh and clean," her mom had said, satisfied. And Oak hadn't thought to question it. After all, she hadn't even wanted to move in the first place; why would she care how the new place was painted?

Looking around Alder's home, Oak felt suddenly very

sorry that she hadn't insisted on color. For color was everywhere here: the entry hall was a butter yellow; the table near the door was lavender; an assortment of colorfully striped hats and scarves crowded the hooks nearby, and a basket on the floor overflowed with balls of yarn and knitting needles.

Still cradling Walnut, Oak followed Alder into the living room. Her heart felt pierced through with envy; it was a riotous, joyous comfort of colors and textures and *things*. Here, the walls were painted a gentle blue. In the center of the room was a long, bright pink velvet couch, slightly sagging in the middle. Three afghan blankets were strewn across it, one in zigzags of bright pinks and purples and greens; another, a series of squares in every color of the rainbow, banded together by black; the third, all plum.

There was an overstuffed bookshelf with too much to take in all at once: books and knickknacks and pieces of pottery, a stuffed animal and a couple of succulents, candles. These books, she noticed, didn't seem to be arranged in any order at all—not by subject, or color, or height. They were stacked and leaned in a mishmash mess that would probably make her mother's eye twitch if she ever saw it.

Next to Alder's couch was an enormous waxy green fern, so large that it practically swallowed the short table on which it perched. In Oak's arms, Walnut struggled to get loose, so she bent down and set him on the floor. The kitten made a beeline for the fern and stood up on his hind legs to sniff it.

Alder's kitten—who, Oak now realized, must be named after this plant—watched as her brother explored a bit. She looked on curiously as Walnut peered underneath the couch, as he reached for and batted at a ball of yarn that must have escaped from the basket in the front hall.

"Does your mom knit a lot?" Oak asked.

Alder shrugged and blushed red. "We both do," he said.

"That's pretty cool," said Oak, and she walked farther into the house, through the kitchen (painted apple green) and into the dining room (violet). There she found more books and puzzles and stacks of papers. She counted seven coffee tins full of pennies and buttons and nails.

She stopped and stared at a portrait on the wall, a picture of a fat dark-haired baby who must have been Alder, and two grown-ups, all posed together beneath an enormous tree. "That's your mom," she said, pointing, "and is that your dad? I've never seen him around."

"That's because he's dead," Alder answered. His voice sounded pinched.

"Oh," said Oak. She looked away from the portrait and she felt, suddenly, her eyes filling with unexpected tears. "I'm sorry."

"That's okay," said Alder. He didn't make eye contact with Oak. "He's been dead since I was little, so I don't really remember him."

That didn't, Oak thought, make it okay, but she understood that it was just a thing that people said, whether it was true or not. "I'm really sorry," she said again, because she wanted Alder to know that she meant it.

After a moment, he looked up at her. "Thanks," he said.

Then Oak returned to looking around, though her heart wasn't in it anymore, and though the feeling she'd had before, of envy, was extinguished. "You have a record player," she said. "I've always wanted to use one of these." She thumbed through the records and pulled one out. *Canary in a Coal Mine*, it was called. The front cover was a picture of a yellow bird in a cage, but the door to the cage was swung open. "May I?" she asked.

Alder shrugged. "Sure."

But Oak found that she wasn't really sure how to make it work, other than sliding the record out of its case and placing it on the turntable. So Alder came over and flipped a switch, and the record began to spin. The arm lifted up and rotated over on top of the spinning record, then dropped down gently so that its needle rubbed against the record's surface, along its tiny grooves. There was a scritch-scratch sound, and then music.

First, a harmonica—one long, high note, held for many moments, and then the tone dropped and a song began. Slowly it stretched out, each note attached to the one before and the one after, like taffy, but sadder. And then another instrument joined in. It sounded sort of like a guitar, but not quite.

"That's a banjo," Alder said, as if he could tell that Oak was wondering.

And then a man's voice, singing.

Way down in the coal mine
Where all men are alone
Way down in the coal mine
Far away from home
Way down in the coal mine
Canary sings his tune
Way down in the coal mine
In the long, dry afternoon

Oak listened, and as she listened, she flipped over the record sleeve. There on the back was a photograph of the singer. He was young, with a thick dark beard and long-ish brown hair brushed back from his forehead. Oak felt a shock of recognition; she looked up to the portrait on the wall and then back down to the record sleeve in her hands. Then she glanced over at Alder to see if he had noticed what she had noticed, but he was staring off as if into space, listening.

Oak turned the record sleeve over again, so the picture of the bird was showing, and she said, "I like the music. It's really good." She set the sleeve down on the table.

Alder smiled, kind of shy. "I like it too," he said, but that was all he said.

When the song was over, Alder flipped the little switch again so that the arm rotated up and away from the record, settling back into its rest, and the record slowed, then stopped.

"Come on," Alder said, heading back into the living room. "I'll introduce you to Mort."

The kittens were entwined amid the unspooled yarn; like rays of floppy sunshine, the soft yellow loops of spun wool danced across the couch, the floor, wrapped around one leg of a chair.

Oak could imagine the fun the kittens had had, and she could picture the path they'd taken, batting the ball of unfurling color under the couch, across the floor, around the leg of the chair, and into a patch of warm sunshine where they had ended their play in a fuzzy pile of yarn and each other. Their eight orange-and-white-striped legs crisscrossed and tangled, their two sweet faces turned toward one another, and one of them, Fern or Walnut—it was impossible to tell which—softly snored.

"Whoa," said Alder, and though that was all he said, Oak nodded. Because she felt certain that he was thinking the same thing she was thinking: look how much fun they have together.

Like it or not, she thought, for the good of the kittens, she and Alder were going to have to be friends.

"Okay," she said. "Tell me about Mort."

Alder pointed up to a shelf full of knickknacks and books. "He's up there," he said.

Oak stepped toward the bookshelf. What she had thought before was a kid's stuffed animal she now saw was something else: a taxidermied opossum, oddly smiling as if it knew the secrets of the universe.

"What . . . ?"

"It was a present from my dad to my mom," Alder said. He was pulling a chair closer to the bookshelf, and he scrambled onto it so he could reach the opossum. "They found it at some weird shop in Seattle, before I was born." He grasped the opossum, gently but firmly, and held it out to Oak. "Here," he said.

She hesitated. Honestly, Oak had no desire to touch that weird dead thing.

"It's not really dead," Alder said. "I mean, it *is* dead. But not, like, rotting."

"Mm-hm," said Oak, and because Alder was still holding it out to her, she took it. It was heavier than she'd expected, and not soft at all like the kittens; the *fur* was soft, but it was solid underneath. "I mean," Oak said, walking over to the couch and sitting down, "it *is* dead. That's its name, after all."

"Its name?" Alder hopped down from the chair.

"Yeah," said Oak.

Alder flinched a little, like maybe Oak's tone made him feel like she thought he was stupid or something.

"I mean," she started again, trying to make her voice gentler, "*Mort* means 'dead.' In French?"

"It does?" said Alder. "Huh."

Now Oak felt bad that she'd told him.

"I always thought it was, like, short for Morty."

"Totally." Oak nodded.

"Except," Alder said, more to himself than to Oak, "it makes way more sense that they named it Mort because it means 'dead' than because it's short for Morty. Since it's . . . dead."

Alder looked deflated, like he was being forced to reevaluate something he'd always seen one way, as something else.

"Anyway," said Oak, "it doesn't really matter *why* they named him Mort, does it? What matters really is what the heck *happened* yesterday! There was a giant talking rat—"

"Opossum," interjected Alder.

"A giant talking opossum," Oak corrected, forcing herself to stay calm, "and we were in his *house*. A house that wasn't there two seconds before, and a house that wasn't there two seconds after we left."

"Yeah," said Alder, but he didn't sound convinced.

"What's the matter?" Oak said.

"I've been thinking," said Alder, "maybe . . . we imagined it."

"Imagined it *together*?" Oak was finding it increasingly difficult to regulate her tone.

"Yeah," said Alder. "Doesn't that happen sometimes? Like, maybe we were both sick with the same virus? Or maybe we were both exposed to, like, the same toxin? Maybe we ate something weird. What did you have for lunch yesterday?"

"Peanut butter and jelly sandwich and an apple," Oak said. "I brought it from home."

"Oh," said Alder, deflated. "I had the school pizza. Cheese."

Oak could see him struggling to come up with another explanation for what had happened, for what they had seen. She'd done the same thing, she supposed, while they were in Mort's house; she'd thought maybe she had been struck by lightning and had fallen into a coma or something. But now they were back home, safe and sound, and it was clear they had *been somewhere else*. Oak was positively itching to figure out where, exactly, that was, and how they could have gotten there. Why didn't Alder just want to admit it— they had experienced something extraordinary, something truly bizarre? Then they could try to figure out what had happened. And what might happen next.

She opened her mouth to explain all of this, to *make* Alder understand, but just then they heard a car turn into the driveway.

"We'll talk about it later, okay?" said Alder. "That's my mom. I don't want her to know."

At least they agreed about something. "I didn't tell my mom either," Oak said. "No reason for them to worry until we figure out what's going on. For now, we can tell your mom we're working on our school project, okay? We probably should anyway."

Alder nodded and went to get his notebook from his backpack. "Family," he said, flipping through the pages until he found his notes from class. He sat down on the floor, across from Oak, and rested his notebook on the coffee table. "We could start with the kittens," he suggested. "They're part of our families now, but they're also related to each other."

"And that sort of makes us family, too, doesn't it?" said Oak. "Not in-laws, but . . . something?"

"Something," said Alder, nodding. "It makes us something."

CHAPTER 15

"You'll never believe who I ran into at the library," called Alder's mom as she pushed through the front door. "Mr. Winderby. Remember him? From the yarn store that shut down last year?"

"Uh-huh," said Alder. "Mom—" He was going to introduce Oak, but she continued.

"Well, he remembers *you*," she said, shrugging off her sweater and setting down her purse and a box full of books near the front door. "He couldn't stop going on about what a talented young man you are, which, of course, he didn't need to tell *me*. Anyway, he and his wife are doing fine, he says, still knitting, and he says they're thinking about maybe opening another storefront in the next year or—"

Finally, Mom turned toward the living room and noticed that they had company.

"Oh!" Alder's mom said. "Hello!"

"Hi," said Oak.

"Mom," Alder said, "this is Oak, from school. Oak, this is my mom. Her name is Greta."

"Nice to meet you," said Oak, and Alder was impressed by her manners, the way she stood up and held out her hand.

Alder's mom shook it and smiled. "Nice to meet you, too," she said.

Then she noticed the unspooled yarn, and Alder watched her gaze follow it around the chair leg, under the couch, and to the orange sleepy lump of kittens tangled in it.

"What's this?" she said. "Two kittens?"

"Mom," said Alder, "it's the craziest thing! Oak and her mom adopted Fern's brother! Isn't that amazing!"

"That *is* amazing," said Mom. "What are the chances?"

She looked at them both with a big, wondrous smile, and Alder could tell that she was happy he had a friend over. Though they hadn't really talked about it, Alder knew that she had noticed he'd been lonely, and that Marcus hadn't been around at all.

"And," said Alder, "what's even cooler is that Walnut lives right next door!"

His mom looked confused.

"I mean," said Alder, "Oak and her parents bought the house next door. So Fern and Walnut—that's the kitten's name—they are neighbors, too. And—"

Alder's sentence petered out as he watched Mom's expression shift—her wide-open smile at the wonder of the kitten coincidence faded away, and she looked, for a moment, almost angry. But then it was like a mask slipped across her features, sort of pleasant but rigid, as if it were Mom's face still but also, oddly, a stranger's.

"The world is full of coincidences," Mom said, and her voice, too, sounded like it was wearing a mask. "Oak, it's nice to meet you. Alder," she said, turning to him, "when you have a moment, will you help me with something in the kitchen?"

And then she passed through the living room and disappeared into the kitchen, not even stopping to scratch Fern's head.

Alder felt itchy and uncomfortable as he turned back to Oak. He was embarrassed, he realized, by the way his mother was acting. It wasn't like her to be cold to *anyone*, and especially not a kid, and double especially not a kid who Alder had over as a guest.

Oak's face looked normal, like maybe she hadn't noticed that his mom had been rude to her. Oak didn't know his mom, Alder told himself, so she had nothing to compare his mother's behavior to. Probably he was the only one who'd noticed the way his mom had shifted.

But then Oak leaned forward and whispered, "That was weird, wasn't it?"

Alder nodded, miserable. "I'll be right back," he said. And he followed his mom into the kitchen. There, he found her standing in front of the sink, her hands resting on the countertop. She stared out the window at the side of Oak's house. Her eyes were unblinking.

"Mom," said Alder, a half whisper. "What was that about? Why are you being weird?"

It was a long moment before Mom turned her head toward Alder, and when she did, he was shocked to see that her face was damp with tears. "I'm sorry, buddy," she said. She wiped her face with her hands. "I guess I'm just not feeling well. That's all."

Alder felt, in a rapid series of flashes, shocked and then worried and then scared. "Are you sick?" he asked. "Are you going to be okay?"

"Oh, no, no, it's nothing like that," Mom said, and she was herself again, suddenly, the person who took care of Alder, the warm tall force that made everything all right. She crossed the kitchen and took him in her arms, pulled him into an embrace. "I'm *fine*, Alder, really I am. The picture of health. I just had a . . . a *moment*, that's all. It's nothing. I promise," she said, and she kissed his head.

Alder pulled away a little so he could see her face. Her eyes were red, a little, but they crinkled up in the corners the way they should, in a smile. She didn't look sick, and the strange impression that she was wearing a mask was completely gone. He felt his stomach unclench, and he hugged his mom again.

"Okay," he said, and then he stepped away. "What did you need help with?"

"Oh," Mom said, and she waved her hand as if shooing a fly. "It's nothing. I don't even remember. Go on, get back to work. You have an hour or so until dinner."

"All right," said Alder, feeling comfortable again. "Is it okay if I ask Oak to stay to eat with us?"

"No," said Mom. The word came out quickly, like a bark, like a bolt, and Alder flinched. "Not tonight," she added, softening her tone. "I hadn't counted on three for dinner."

"Okay," said Alder, and he headed back to the living room, to Oak and the kittens.

It was the first time Alder could remember his mom ever, ever saying no to inviting someone to stay for dinner.

Though he returned to the living room and tried to make some progress on the "family" project, Alder's heart wasn't in it. He was embarrassed about how his mom had acted, and he couldn't get her expression out of his head.

Oak seemed to feel the change in the room. It wasn't too long before she said, "Well, I'd better be getting home," and Alder didn't try to convince her to stay. She woke up Walnut by untangling him from the yarn, and he made a little mew of protest as she lifted him from where he lay, entwined with Fern. "Come on, little guy," she said to the kitten, and then, to Alder, "I'll see you tomorrow."

*　*　*

The next day was Friday, and Alder wasn't really in the mood to talk to anyone, but especially not Beck. Once again, Beck had been sitting next to Marcus on the bus, and once again, Marcus had done that stupid thing where he lifted his chin in Alder's direction as Alder slumped down the aisle toward the back of the bus. Marcus had learned that chin thing from Beck, Alder was sure, and it seemed like a little twist of the knife each time he did it. The knife being Beck stealing Alder's friend.

But when, at ten o'clock that morning, Mr. Rivera said it was time to work on their projects, there was Beck, looming large over Alder's desk, his blond hair swinging forward as he stared down.

"'Sup," said Beck.

"'Sup," said Alder.

"We're water partners," Beck said.

"Uh-huh." They might as well get this over with, and so he pulled out his notebook. He'd done as much of the water research on his own as possible, hoping not to have to spend too much time with Beck.

He flipped open to the section labeled WATER.

There, he'd made a list:

Language Arts
History
Current Events
PE

Math

Art

Science

And next to each topic, he'd begun to brainstorm things they could research about water. For math, he'd put down the word "Eureka."

Beck pointed to it. "Eureka? Like, the town?"

"No," said Alder. "Like, the word."

Beck had brought his chair over to Alder's desk, and now he flipped around and sat in it backward. "I don't get it," he said. "What does Eureka have to do with water?"

Beck even *sat* cool. "Do you know about Archimedes?" Alder asked.

Beck shook his head.

"Well," said Alder, feeling a little glad that he knew something that Beck didn't, "Archimedes was a mathematician in ancient Greece. And he was given a problem to solve, by the king. See, the king had hired a goldsmith to make a crown for him, solid gold. But when the crown was delivered, the king sort of suspected that maybe the goldsmith had cheated him. So he asked Archimedes to figure out if it was pure gold or if it was actually a little bit of gold mixed with another metal, like silver. But the problem was that he liked the crown, and he didn't want Archimedes to mess with it, or, like, break it or anything."

"How do you spell Archimedes?" asked Beck, pulling out his phone.

Alder told him, then continued. "Anyway, Archimedes didn't know how to solve the problem. How can you figure out what something is made of if you can't open it up and look inside? But then, one day, he was taking a bath."

"Do adults really take baths?" asked Beck, typing something into his phone. "The last time I took a bath I think I was like four years old."

"Yeah," said Alder, hoping Beck wouldn't look up and see how red he'd turned, "me too. But anyway, Archimedes wasn't in his own bathroom or anything. He was in a public bathhouse. I guess that's how everyone got clean back then. And he was getting into the bathtub, and he noticed how the water sloshed out. And he realized that the more of his body he put underwater, the higher the water around him rose up, and the more sloshed out. And he realized that he could figure out, using math and water, whether the crown was made of solid gold or whether it was silver with a gold coating. All he had to do, he figured, was weigh the crown and then see if a solid lump of gold that weighed the same as the crown sloshed out the same amount of water. If it did, then the crown was solid gold. If it didn't, that meant the king had been cheated. See?"

"Mm-hmm," said Beck, but he was doing something on his phone—flipping through something with his thumb.

133

Alder felt himself getting mad. Here he was giving Beck the perfect example of water and math for their project, and Beck couldn't even *pretend* to pay attention.

Alder heard his voice grow louder. "So *anyway*," he said, "Archimedes jumped out of his bath and he ran—totally naked!—through the town. And he shouted—"

"Eureka!" said Beck, looking up from his phone with a grin.

"Um. Yeah. Eureka," said Alder. I thought you didn't know the story."

"I didn't," Beck said. He showed Alder his phone. "I just looked it up. But this article says that it probably isn't true—that part about running naked through town yelling 'Eureka.' It says some other dude started telling that story, like, two hundred years later."

Alder took the phone and read through the article. Beck was right. "Oh," he said, defeated.

"It's still a really good story, though," said Beck, taking back the phone when Alder was done and sticking it into his pocket. "And it is about math and water. Great job, Alder. Let's use it."

Alder grinned. And then he had an idea. Maybe, if he could get Beck to be his friend, then the three of them—him, Beck, and Marcus—could hang out together. It wouldn't be as good as having Marcus all to himself, but it would be better than nothing. And Beck *had* offered to walk with him to the nurse's office the other day. "Hey," he said, "maybe we can get together again after school. You know, to work some more together."

Beck shook his head. "Cross-country club," he said. "We're doing a whole 5K today."

"Maybe we could sit together at lunch—" Alder started to say, but then Mr. Rivera stood up from his desk.

"Okay, friends, time to rotate. Wrap it up."

And just like that, Beck was gone.

CHAPTER 16

It turned out that lunch from the cafeteria wasn't actually as good as lunch from home, which was a disappointment. First, Oak had to wait in line to buy it, which took close to ten minutes. Then, as she made her way across the lunchroom with her tray, someone bumped into her and some of her tomato soup sloshed out of its bowl. Then, when she finally made it to the table where she sat each day with Cynthia, Cameron, Carmen, and Miriam, she noticed that they had all brought lunch from home today.

"Word to the wise," said Cynthia, unwrapping her sandwich. "Never buy lunch on Fridays. It's always leftovers."

"Good to know," said Oak. She tried the tomato soup. Not quite warm enough, and way too salty.

"This weekend," said Cameron, "we're going apple picking!"

"And pumpkin picking," said Carmen, who had cut bangs, much to Oak's relief. It had made Oak so uncomfortable to never quite be 100 percent sure which twin she was talking to.

"Fun," said Miriam. She'd brought enchiladas from home in a little glass dish, and she'd used the cafeteria microwave to heat them up. They looked way better than anything else on the table. "We're going to go visit my brother in Arizona."

"You have a brother in Arizona?" Oak asked.

Miriam nodded. "He's eight years older than me, and he moved away to college two months ago. We haven't seen him since he left."

"Wow," said Cynthia. "Do you miss him?"

Miriam shrugged. "I guess so," she said. "I don't have to share the bathroom anymore, which is nice. And he says that now he has to share a bathroom with five other guys!" She grinned.

Oak sighed, giving up on her lunch, and set down her spoon. As she did, she saw Alder, lunch bag in hand, scanning the cafeteria as if he were lost.

"Alder!" she called, waving.

He looked over in her direction, but when Oak motioned for him to come join their table, he looked away and wandered toward the far end of the room.

"My parents are making me go hiking on Saturday," Cynthia was telling the table. "Even though I told them I'm allergic to nature."

Everyone laughed, and Oak laughed along with them, but inside she was thinking about Alder. There was no way he hadn't heard her.

After school, Oak climbed onto the bus. There was Alder, in a window seat. She flopped down next to him. He looked up, surprised.

"Hey," she said.

"Hey," he answered. He looked around, like he was searching for someone.

"Are you saving this seat for someone?" Oak asked.

"Um. No," said Alder, but he looked like maybe he was.

"I can move," Oak said.

"That's okay," said Alder.

A minute later, they were on their way.

"So," said Oak, but she didn't know what to say after that. She wanted to talk more about Mort and his house, but the bus wasn't exactly the best place to speculate if they wanted to keep it to themselves.

"Sew buttons," said Alder.

"What?"

"Sorry," said Alder. "It's just an expression. Someone

says 'So,' and then you say 'Sew buttons.'" He shrugged. "It's stupid."

"No," said Oak. "It's not stupid. I've just never heard it before."

Then she didn't know what to say again. It was weird that she felt uncomfortable; it was just yesterday that they had been hanging out at Alder's house, and just the day before that when they had found themselves in a secret house with an impossible host. Right now, it seemed equally unbelievable that they had been comfortable with each other yesterday as that they had met a talking opossum the day before.

They passed the bus ride in uncomfortable silence. When they reached Rollingwood Drive and Faith called, "See ya, tree kids!" both Oak and Alder mumbled their goodbyes.

Maybe now that they were off the bus, they could talk some more about Mort, Oak thought, but Alder sped up, like he wasn't in the mood.

"Well, see you," he said as he turned to head up the path to his front door, but Oak called, "Hey, wait!"

Alder stopped.

"Hey," Oak said again. "Why did you ignore me today in the cafeteria?"

"Ignore you?" Alder said.

"Yes," said Oak. "When I called your name and waved

you over to our table. How come you didn't join us?"

"Oh," said Alder. "That. Well, it's nothing personal."

"Whenever anyone says that," Oak answered, "it's always personal."

"No," said Alder, "it's not. It's just—I mean, it was nice of you to invite me to sit with you and your friends. But. I mean—"

"*What?*" Oak felt herself growing angry, though she didn't know what she was angry about yet.

"Well," said Alder, "I don't know exactly. I was kind of hoping someone else was going to ask me to sit with him at lunch, I guess."

"It's not because we were all *girls*, was it?" Oak asked.

"No," said Alder quickly. Then, "But, I don't know, maybe it *would* be . . . weird . . . for me to sit at a table with all girls."

Oak felt her face turning red, just the way her mother's face sometimes got when *she* was mad. Alder must have noticed, because he spoke more quickly now, like his words were trying to outrun a wildfire. "It's nothing personal," he said again.

Oak was mad enough to spit, but she didn't let herself yell. In fact, her voice got quieter. "Darla sits at a table with her Dungeons and Dragons friends, and they're all boys. Is *that* weird?"

"That's different," said Alder quickly.

But when Oak asked, "How?" Alder didn't have a reason.

"It just is," he said.

Oak turned away from him and toward her house.

"Want to get the kittens together this weekend?" Alder called after her.

Oak didn't answer. She just slammed her door behind her.

The rain came back that night, but gently. No wind; no bright flashes of lightning. No ominous rumbles of thunder. It fell, misty and silent, all night long and most of Saturday. Oak spent the day inside, mostly in her room, with Walnut.

She sat on her bed and looked out the window into the damp gray day. The rain was so light that she couldn't hear it falling, and at some angles, she couldn't see it falling, either. But if she adjusted her eyes and paid better attention, then there it was, like a screen, barely there but still absolutely there, also.

Walnut seemed content to cuddle, curled into a round orange ball in her lap. Not really a ball, Oak thought, stroking the kitten from head to rump. More like the frond of a fern that has not yet unfurled. She had seen many such fern fronds at home in San Francisco, and thinking about them now made Oak aware of the fact that it had been a few days since she'd felt truly homesick. For better or for worse, this felt like home now, this house and this street and this school.

Soon, her dad would be moving down permanently, and then it would become all the way home.

And thinking of fern fronds made Oak think, also, of Fern. Walnut's sister. How very strange it was that her kitten and Alder's kitten had both found their way outside during a storm, and that they had both somehow made their way into that house that wasn't there . . . though, as she moved further away from that strange incident, even Oak was having a more and more difficult time remaining convinced that it had truly occurred.

Wasn't there a book that she'd seen somewhere? About cats? Where was it . . . was it at school? That didn't seem right. Was it at Alder's house, maybe?

No. Oak remembered.

Trying not to wake Walnut, Oak scooched him off her lap so she could stand. Walnut made a sound like he was a bit disgruntled, and he shifted position, but then he fell back into noodly sleep.

The book had been black, that she knew. She remembered this because when she had arranged the shelf in a rainbow of spines, this book had belonged on the very bottom shelf, far to the right. It was the book her father had given her mother years ago, the one he'd gotten on that business trip up to Washington State.

Black, with gold lettering. What had the words read? *Feline* . . . something.

Of course, since her mom had rearranged all the work Oak had done to make the books into a rainbow, the book would no longer be in the bottom right corner. Still, Oak checked there first, just in case.

No luck. That shelf held a series of short story collections, all books from Oak's father's college days.

Hmm.

Oak took a step back to scan the shelves as a whole. Maybe the book would stick out in some way.

No.

So Oak decided to begin at the beginning. She scanned her eyes along each row, from the top left to the bottom right, sure she would see the book if she looked for it that way.

Still, no.

Now Oak felt a little nervous. Could the book have disappeared, like Walnut had?

She moved the ottoman over to the bookshelf and climbed atop it. *Begin at the beginning*, she told herself, and so she did, making sure to touch each and every book one by one.

It took the better part of half an hour, but eventually Oak found herself, yet again, crouched down by the bookshelf's bottom right corner. She felt a sight twitch in her eye.

"Mom!" she yelled.

"Don't yell, come find me!" Mom yelled back.

Oak put a hand up to her eyelid and held it still. But when she brought her hand down again, the twitch was still there.

Oak found her mother in the third bedroom, which she had converted to a home office for days when she worked from home or when she still had work to do after business hours. She was sitting at her computer; there were blueprints on the screen, plans for a mini-mall that her architecture firm had been hired to design. "What do you need, my love?" she asked, but she didn't look up from her work.

"I'm looking for a book, and I can't find it," Oak said. She didn't mention that the reason she couldn't find it was that her mother had reordered the bookshelves.

"Did you look carefully?"

"Yes," said Oak. "Twice."

Then she waited for her mother to reply, but her mother seemed to get lost in her work, forgetting that Oak was even there. Insulting.

Oak cleared her throat, loudly, and when that didn't work, she jostled her mother's chair.

"Oops," Oak said. "Sorry."

At last, Oak's mother swiveled around. She ran her hand across her short hair the way she liked to do when she was thinking. "Let's see," she said. "I suppose it could have ended up in the giveaway box."

"What giveaway box?"

"The library was doing a fundraiser; I saw a sign. A book sale. We had more books than we needed, they needed books, voilà."

"But I *need* this book," Oak said. "And you never asked me, Mom."

What she wanted to say—what she didn't say—was that her mother never asked her *anything*. Not about books. Not about bookshelves. Not about moving. Oak felt tempted to say all of this, but right now, the book was the important thing.

"What book was it?" Mom asked.

"I don't remember the title," Oak admitted.

"Well, what's it about?"

"I don't *know*, exactly," Oak said. Her voice went up an octave.

Mom laughed. "So you don't remember the title, and you don't know what it's about, but you *need* this book?"

Oak didn't say anything. There was no point, when her mom got like this. For some reason, Oak didn't want to tell her mom that the book was the one her dad had brought home from that business trip. Her mom shouldn't have forgotten; she shouldn't have given it away. It was a gift. From Dad.

Maybe Mom noticed that Oak was upset, because she

stopped laughing and cleared her throat. "Well," she said, "hmm. I suppose we could go over to the library and see if they still have it. I'm not sure when the book sale is happening. I could take you . . . tomorrow?"

Oak did not want to wait until tomorrow. "I'll go myself," she grumbled. "I'll ride my bike."

"Wear your helmet, and be careful," Mom said, turning back to her work. "It's wet out there."

Oak turned away, so angry she felt like punching something, or someone. If her mother had just left the bookshelf the way Oak had arranged it, then Oak wouldn't have to ride her bike all alone in the rain to the library. If her mother *ever* listened to her, or cared what she thought, they wouldn't even be in this dumb city.

A little voice inside her head tried to remind Oak that if they weren't in this dumb city, she wouldn't have ever met little Walnut, but Oak did not feel like listening to that voice, not now.

She yanked open the front door. Before she went outside, she turned back and yelled, "I want to paint my room! I hate white walls!"

With that, she slammed the door.

It *was* wet outside, but at least it wasn't raining anymore. Oak pulled her bicycle from the garage, strapped on her helmet, and zipped up her jacket. She glanced over at Alder's house and considered, for a moment, inviting him to go with her. It would be nice to have company. But then she remembered how he'd ignored her in the cafeteria, and how he'd tried to explain it. She turned away and headed up the street, standing as she pumped her bike up the hill.

It was just over a mile and a half to the library, and by the time Oak arrived, she felt much better. The cold, clear air felt good on her skin and in her lungs, and it felt good to move her legs and push herself. And it was exciting, too, to be exploring a new place like this all on her own. Oak found herself wondering why she'd waited so long to venture away from her new neighborhood; back in San Francisco, she'd walked all over the place by herself—to Stacia's apartment, to school, to her old library and three different parks and the ice cream place during the summer. Here, things were more spread out, and barely anyone seemed to walk or bike *anywhere*. Everyone either rode the bus or got a ride to school, and other than people dressed in tight-fitting clothes, speed walking or jogging for exercise, nobody seemed to use the sidewalks.

So by the time she arrived at the library, a bit out of breath but feeling rather pleased with herself, Oak's eye had stopped twitching and she was feeling quite confident. She marched straight up to the circulation desk, unlatching her helmet as she went.

"Hello," she said to the man behind the counter.

He blinked up at her, a book in his hands. "Hello," he said. "Can I help you?"

"I need to find a book," she said.

The man chuckled and spread his arms out wide. "You're in the right place."

"No, a specific book," Oak said, and then, before he could make another joke, she rushed on. "My mother accidentally donated a book from home for your book sale. And she didn't know that I needed it. But I do."

"Oh," said the man. His smile faded.

"It's okay if I have to buy it back," Oak rushed on. "I mean, I guess it's for a good cause, and I brought my allowance, so if I have to, I'll buy it."

"No," said the man. "It's not that."

"What, then?" The good, powerful, I-can-do-anything energy Oak had been feeling was slipping away.

"It's just—well, the sale was this week, Monday through Friday. Yesterday was the last day, you see."

"Oh," said Oak, feeling desperate. "Well, maybe no one bought my book. Where are the leftovers? I'll look through them, if that's all right."

"You don't understand," the man said. He looked very sorry. Sincerely sorry. "There are no leftover books. The remainders were picked up this morning. They've been taken to recycling. But maybe we have a copy of the book in our stacks!" He said this last bit encouragingly, trying to soften the blow, it seemed. "I'm happy to help you look."

Oak took a step back, away from the counter. "I don't remember the title," she said.

"Well, what's it about? We can look it up that way, too." The man pressed the button on his mouse to bring his computer to life.

Oak shook her head. All she remembered about the book was that it had the word "Feline" in the title, and that it had been a black book with gold embossed lettering. Surely that was not enough to go on.

"That's okay," she said, even though it really wasn't. "Thanks anyway."

The ride home was mostly downhill. An easy ride. It should have been fun, and Oak should have had a book tucked into her jacket's inner pocket.

But it wasn't. And she didn't.

CHAPTER 17

Alder spent the whole weekend feeling like a jerk.

On Saturday he paced around his house mumbling "idiot, idiot, jerk" to himself. Fern sat on the pink velvet couch, watching him curiously. He only left the house once, to run errands with his mom. At least they stopped by the drugstore and picked up a DNA kit for the school project. Filling the little vial with spit (which was disgusting), Alder thought maybe this would help a little with Oak being mad at him.

Sunday, Alder lay flat on his back on his bedroom floor for a good part of the morning, staring up at a water stain on his ceiling.

"She should understand that it's different for boys," he told himself.

But the words, said out loud, felt not right.

He thought about Darla, and what Oak had said about her—"Darla sits at a table with her Dungeons and Dragons friends, and they're all boys. Is *that* weird?"

His immediate response had been that no, of course *that* wasn't weird. What he hadn't said was what he felt inside. It was fine that Darla was like one of the guys. The fact that she was a girl who played Dungeons & Dragons after school every day, that she always wore a baseball cap, and that, for her last birthday, she had invited four of her best friends, all boys, to spend the afternoon at Comic Con, where they'd all had their picture taken together in front of an enormous poster of the new movie based on that game *Starfield*, all of that was perfectly fine.

But him, sitting at a table full of *girls*?

That made Alder feel . . . nervous.

And feeling nervous about the possibility of sitting at a table of all girls made Alder feel bad. About himself.

"Jerk, jerk, jerk," he said, rolling over onto his stomach and banging his forehead against the floor.

But not sitting with Oak and her friends wasn't only about the girl-boy thing. The truth was that each day at lunch, Alder hoped that Marcus would want to eat with him. That there would be an empty seat next to Marcus and, just like old times, he would wave Alder over as if it was no big deal at all, and they would sit together and joke about things. Nothing special, but still somehow completely special. There it was again—the way something could be two opposite things in the same moment.

Anyway, if Alder sat with Oak and her friends, that would be like giving up hope. It would be admitting that Marcus didn't want to be his friend anymore.

Alder rolled the other way, onto his back, and stared up at the ceiling.

Fern hopped down from the bed to see what he was doing. She purred and pushed her head into his arm. Fern didn't think he was a jerk, Alder comforted himself.

But, another voice said that was just because Fern didn't know.

Alder stood. He picked up Fern and wandered to his window. He looked over at Oak's house. The addition above the garage was coming along; it had walls now, though they weren't yet covered in stucco. Today was a Sunday, so the construction workers weren't there.

Then Alder's gaze fell to the tree stump. He sighed. It had been a beautiful tree. But he realized that, though he was still sad about it, he wasn't angry anymore. He wondered when, exactly, that had changed.

Fern perked up, as if she saw something interesting. She made a little sound like he'd heard her do when she saw a fly, a cross between a meow and a growl. A meowl. Alder took another step toward the window so his forehead pressed against the cold glass pane.

"What is it, girl?" he asked. He squinted and focused, trying to see what Fern saw.

Nothing.

He relaxed his gaze and gave up. And that was when he saw it—a glint, a glimmer, a shimmer.

Fern seemed to know when Alder saw it, for she meowled again, as if she were saying, "Finally! What took you so long?"

Alder tried to memorize what he was seeing—or what he *thought* he was seeing—but as soon as he focused in and looked directly at the spot, the shimmer disappeared. He softened his gaze again, letting the world slip out of focus . . . and there it was. The trick seemed to be not to look directly at it, whatever it was.

Doing his best to keep his eyes loose, Alder set Fern on his bed and left his room, heading for the front door. He heard Fern jump down from the bed, he heard her padding behind him. Not bothering to put on shoes, Alder cracked open the front door and slipped outside. Fern yowled crossly when he shut her in, but Alder ignored her. He wasn't about to risk losing his kitten again.

Shoes would have been a good idea. Alder had regrets as he picked his way through the damp grass. The ground felt a little squishy too, in a way that made Alder think of worms. Alder was not a fan of worms or wormy things. Not even spaghetti. But he pressed on, in spite of the dampness, in spite of the squish, in spite of the images of worms in his head. As he did, he tried his best to keep his gaze soft and gently scanned the area around the tree stump, looking for the patch of shimmer.

When he couldn't find it, Alder decided to walk in a circle all around the stump. Maybe he would see it from a different angle. Slowly, Alder circled the stump. Gently, Alder scanned the air. Gingerly, Alder stepped through the grass.

But nothing. Frustrated, Alder sighed. He felt his gaze harden back into normal.

There—just in his periphery—a flash! Could it be that the shimmer had moved over there? Alder turned his head to pinpoint what he'd seen out of the corner of his eye.

Oh. It wasn't the shimmer. It was the front window of Oak's house, and the movement he'd seen was Oak herself, peering out, watching him.

Alder lifted his hand in a wave. Oak stared at him, and though they were separated by the length of the yard and the pane of her window, Alder had no problem at all reading her expression.

Without a wave in return or an acknowledgment of any kind, Oak turned away.

Falteringly, Alder lowered his hand. His stomach felt sick again. "Idiot, idiot, jerk," he berated himself, and he headed back inside.

"Alder," his mom called from the kitchen, "you've been

moping around all weekend! How about we start a new puzzle—does that sound like fun?"

Alder shook his head. He didn't feel like doing anything.

"Well," said his mom, "why don't you look through that box of books and craft stuff I brought home from the donation fair? Maybe you'll find something interesting."

Alder didn't feel like looking at books, either, but Mom said, "Either you find something to do or I will," so he begrudgingly made his way to the box.

The next morning, Alder waited outside Oak's house so he could apologize. He'd even brought her something from the book box, as a sort of peace offering. He waited for what felt like a long time, but when Oak still hadn't emerged five minutes before the bus was due to arrive, Alder had no choice but to head for the corner.

"Just one tree kid today, huh?" said Faith.

"I guess so." Alder began to head up the aisle.

"Did you kids ever find that house?" she asked.

Alder stopped dead in his tracks. "What did you say?"

"You know," Faith said. "You're in number Eleven. Tree girl lives in number Fifteen. But where's the missing house? Where is number Thirteen? Did you find it yet?"

She was joking around. Alder could tell from her smile, the loose and happy tone in her voice.

"No," he answered slowly. "Not yet."

155

By the time Mr. Rivera called the class to order, Oak had not arrived. This was particularly inconvenient for Alder, as they jumped right into their interdisciplinary project and he was supposed to be paired with her today.

"It's tough to go it alone without your family," Mr. Rivera said, mustache twitching.

"Huh?" Alder said, confused.

Mr. Rivera tapped the open page in Alder's notebook, which was headed with the word *Family*, followed by a hodgepodge of notes.

"Oh," said Alder. "Right."

Mr. Rivera wandered away, making encouraging jokes and checking on progress as he went up the aisle.

The least he could do, Alder thought, was make some progress in Oak's absence. But before he even looked at his notes, he found himself immediately distracted by that phrase . . . *the least he could do*. It was a funny thing to aim for, wasn't it? The *least* that someone could do? Why not aim for the *most* that someone could do? Or, maybe, the middle amount?

Alder had always liked language and words. Maybe it was something he'd gotten from his dad. Writing songs, after all, is about playing with words and the ways they fit together, with meaning and rhythm and rhyme.

Alder shook his head to clear it. Here he was, allowing himself to focus on the wrong thing. He was supposed to be focused on *family*, and yet he was thinking about . . . well, actually, he *was* thinking about family. His family. His dad.

He laughed a little. Wasn't that funny? That he tried to think about one thing and then found himself thinking about another thing, but then it turned out that the other thing really was the first thing after all? He wished he had someone to share that with. Glumly, Alder looked around. He wished Oak were here.

It took Alder three attempts to approach Oak's lunch table before he finally went through with it.

The first time Alder tried to approach their table, he couldn't even bring himself to slow down as he passed it. He just kept walking, as if he suddenly saw someone on the far end of the cafeteria who was waiting for him.

On the second pass, Alder did manage to slow down. Oak wasn't there, of course, but the others were—Cynthia and Miriam from his class, and the twins, who were in the other fifth grade class and whose names, he realized, he didn't know. He even cast a friendly smile in the table's general direction, but none of the girls seemed to notice. They were all leaning forward, looking at pictures on one of the twins' phones. Alder didn't *mean* to peek—he knew that was rude—but he couldn't help but notice the picture that was up when he passed, of the twins and a third, younger kid and a couple of grown-ups, with a big basket of fruit, maybe apples, in the photo as well.

On the third pass, Alder forced himself to stop walking when he had reached the table. He counted down—*three steps, two steps, one step*—and then he brought his right foot up to meet his left, and he stopped, just behind the twin with bangs.

"Hello, Alder," said Cynthia. "This is the second time you've passed our table. Do you need something?"

He felt an enormous wave of relief that Cynthia had only noticed him circle the table twice.

"Actually," said Miriam, sipping orange juice, "it's his third."

Miriam.

Alder cleared his throat, though it didn't need clearing. "Hey," he said. "I was just . . . wondering . . . if maybe I could sit here? With you?"

He watched the four girls look at one another as if they were taking a silent vote. It couldn't have taken more than a few seconds, but it felt like ages before Cynthia said, "Sure. Why not?"

It was, Alder knew, a rhetorical question, and he threaded his legs over the bench and sat down. "Thanks," he said, and opened his lunch.

The girls returned to the photos on the phone.

"So how many different kinds of apples did you get?"

Cynthia asked the twins.

"Just three," said the twin holding the phone, the one with bangs. "There were five kinds in the orchard, but our baby brother got cranky before we made it to all of them. And Cameron says we picked more than we could ever eat anyway."

Ah. The other twin was Cameron. One name down, one to go.

"I brought some to share," said Cameron, unzipping her backpack. "And Carmen labeled them so we'd know which is which."

Bingo, thought Alder, feeling rather pleased with himself. The twin with bangs was named Carmen.

Well. Cameron and Carmen. That was confusing. He almost made a smart comment, but then decided at the last moment not to. Maybe he'd just listen for a while.

Cameron pulled a half dozen apples out of a paper bag, two of each kind. A little piece of masking tape was stuck to each apple: Fuji; Honeycrisp; Opal.

"Does anyone have a knife?"

No one did. Here was something Alder could do. "I'll go ask the cafeteria lady," he offered, jumping up.

The best she could offer was a dully serrated plastic butter knife, but it was better than nothing.

"Thanks!" Cameron said when he returned, and she began slicing up the apples. When they had been cut into uneven wedges and sorted by type, everyone dug in.

"Let's all try one kind at a time," suggested Carmen, so they all reached for an Opal piece. Alder bit into the sweet, crisp fruit.

"It's really good," Miriam said, and everyone nodded, including Alder.

"Next, let's try Honeycrisp," said Cynthia.

It was at least as delicious as the Opal. But better even than the tasting, Alder felt, was the tasting *together*.

Finally, they all reached for a slice of Fuji. And then Alder heard from behind him, "What's going on?"

He turned, with a cheekful of apple. There was Oak.

CHAPTER 18

Alder sure did look comfortable at her lunch table with her friends, thought Oak. He had his lunch spread out in front of him and was chummily tasting apple slices, presumably from Carmen and Cameron's trip to the orchard.

"Oak!" said Miriam. "We thought maybe you were sick." She scooted over to make room.

"Dentist appointment," Oak said, stepping over the bench and sitting down. She let her backpack fall on the floor between her feet.

"Want to try some apples?" Carmen offered.

Oak shook her head. "I'm still kind of numb." She rubbed her cheek; she had to remember not to bite herself, the dentist had said. Who had to *remember* not to bite themselves? she had thought, but now, numbed as she was, she had to admit that it was sort of tempting.

"Sorry," said Cameron, biting crisply into a slice.

"Hi," Alder said from across the table. It was the first word he'd spoken to her.

Now, Oak had a decision to make. Doing her best not to chew on the inside of her cheek, she considered: Should she tell the others what Alder had said, about how he'd been embarrassed to sit with them last week, because they were all girls? Should she tell him to go sit somewhere else, that maybe *they* didn't want to sit with *him*?

She could. She could be mean. It would feel *good*, even, to be mean, and Oak was in a bad mood already from the dentist.

Alder looked at her, then down at the table, like he was waiting for her to do it. Waiting for her to tell him she didn't want to sit with him, that none of them did. He even started gathering together his lunch stuff.

And then Oak had a flash of memory: Walnut and Fern cuddled together, wound up in yarn.

"Hey, Alder," Oak said, and her voice sounded mostly sincere. "I'm glad you're sitting with us."

Alder looked up, wide-eyed. It was kind of funny, how surprised he looked. Now Oak smiled.

Alder smiled back cautiously. "Thanks," he said. "Thanks for inviting me the other day."

And then the table felt comfortable again, like a cloud

had been sitting on top of them but now a fresh breeze had blown it away.

"So, did you get a pumpkin?" Oak asked the twins.

"Three of them!" said Cameron. "Each of us got to pick one. Gordie picked the biggest—even Dad couldn't carry it. We had to use a wagon." She reached across the table for another apple slice.

"Oh," said Oak, pointing at her sweater. "You've got a hole there."

"I know." Cameron sighed. She poked at the hole. It was just above the elbow, on the inside, a sort of jagged, small-ish hole in the loosely knit tomato-red sleeve. "And this is my favorite sweater! I wear it practically every day in the fall. It happened when we were picking apples. A branch caught it."

"It wouldn't be hard to stitch that closed," Alder said, comfortably munching another apple slice.

"Yeah, if, like, I knew how to knit," said Cameron.

"Alder does," said Oak. "Maybe he could fix it for you."

"Alder?" said Cameron. "You knit?"

"I mean," said Alder, "Not really. A little."

Oak could tell from the expression on his face, the way he twisted his lips together and looked down at the table again and at the bit of apple in his hand, that he did not want to talk about knitting.

"Could you teach us?" said Miriam. "I've always wanted

to know how to knit."

Alder mumbled something unintelligible.

"What?" said Cynthia loudly. "Speak up!"

Alder cleared his throat. "I guess I could try. I could show you the basics sometime. If you really wanted me to."

"When?" said Cameron. "I don't want this hole to get bigger." She waved her arm in Alder's direction, as if to illustrate the urgency of the matter.

"I don't know . . . maybe you all could come over after school sometime?"

The table began comparing schedules: Cameron and Carmen weren't available until at least Wednesday; Miriam was free tomorrow and Thursday, but not Wednesday; Cynthia had swim practice until six p.m. every afternoon, Monday through Friday, so she couldn't arrange anything until the weekend.

"Just bring some knitting stuff to school tomorrow," suggested Oak. "You can show us how to knit during lunch."

She could tell from Alder's expression that he did *not* like that idea. Of course he didn't; if he'd been weird about sharing a lunch table with girls, he probably wasn't going to be terribly keen on the idea of knitting with them in front of the whole school. But Oak found that she didn't want to take it back. Actually, she was really warming up to the idea of a lunchtime knitting circle. If Alder wanted to sit with them—if he really meant it—then this was a way he could prove it.

"I don't think I have enough knitting needles for everyone," Alder said, rather weakly, Oak thought.

"That's okay," said Cynthia, gathering up her scraps from lunch. The bell was about to ring. "We've got a ton of old knitting stuff from when my mom decided she was going to learn a few years ago. She gave up after a week, but I know where she stashed the supplies. I'll bring a bunch of needles and yarn tomorrow!"

Oak smiled. Just like that, it was settled.

"Hey," said Alder to Oak that afternoon, as they waited for the bus to arrive. "Listen. I'm sorry about the other day. I was a jerk."

Oak shrugged. "Everyone's a jerk sometimes," she said.

"Yeah," said Alder. His hands twisted his backpack straps. "I just—I used to sit with my friend Marcus every day."

"Marcus?" said Oak. "You mean Beck's best friend?"

Alder winced. "Yeah," he said.

Now *Oak* felt like a jerk. "Well, never mind about all that. Listen, do you want to come over? You could bring Fern. We could work on our project . . . and talk some more about Mort."

"Sure," said Alder. "Yeah, okay."

When they got off the bus, he told her he'd be over soon, and Oak went inside. She set down her backpack on the mud bench and slowly kicked off her shoes. Wandering through the rooms, she looked around her house, trying to see them the way a stranger might. She took in the plain white walls; the predictable furniture; the bookshelf, arranged the way bookshelves usually are. Compared to Alder's house, with the clutter and the color and the chaos, Oak's was dreadfully boring.

Well, there was nothing she could do about that now, though she was going to insist on buying some paint for her room. Maybe she could at least set out interesting snacks. And the thought of food made her stomach rumble. She'd skipped lunch because of the dentist, and now it was catching up with her. Also, her mouth was finally un-numb, and that was definitely something to celebrate. She'd make something yummy to share and, she decided with a flash of inspiration, she'd fix a tea tray for the kittens, too!

First, she poked her head into her mom's office.

"Hi," she said. "A kid from school is coming over to work on a project."

"Lovely," said her mom, looking up from her computer and blinking as if she'd spent too many hours staring at it. Oak started to leave, but her mom called out, "Bring me a cup of tea, would you?"

Oak said she would.

There was some smoked salmon in the refrigerator, and cream cheese; she would made little finger sandwiches for herself and Alder, and she would cut little triangles of the salmon for the kittens, arranging them on a saucer. She set to work, humming. When all of that was done, she put on the kettle to boil.

On she hummed as she wiped down the counter, waiting for the kettle to scream. At last it did. Oak poured out a pot of tea for two, and enough cream for four. There were some strawberries, which the kittens probably wouldn't like, and some heart-shaped tuna treats, which she knew for a fact that they would. She filled a small bowl with each.

It was then that Oak realized that she had been humming the song from the other day—the song from Alder's dad's record. She thought about that as she arranged the food and tea things on the table in the front room. She thought about it as she made a mug of tea and delivered it to her mother in her office.

"Thank you," Mom said, and this time when she looked up, she focused for a moment and smiled, which was nice.

Oak smiled back.

"Who's coming over?" Mom asked.

But before Oak could answer, there was a knock on the door. "Gotta get that," said Oak, and she closed her mom's office door so she could work in quiet.

On the porch, in Alder's arms, Fern was arching her back, struggling to break free. Alder was struggling just as much to hold on to her.

"Hey," said Alder.

"Hi," said Oak, grinning. "Your cat looks worked up about something."

"Yeah," said Alder, and he carried the kitten into Oak's house, setting her down as soon as Oak had shut the door. He rubbed a mark on his arm, where he'd been caught by one of the kitten's claws. "She's really interested in that spot by the tree stump. When I walked over here, she went pretty wild trying to get down."

Oak knew exactly the spot Alder was talking about. She nodded. "I've seen Walnut staring out there too," she said. This was something she wanted to talk about more, over tea. "Come on. I made snacks."

Alder came right in, kicking off his shoes when he saw the pile by the door and dumping his backpack on the entry hall floor. But Fern skulked. She sniffed corners and arched her back, careful as she explored the new landscape. Walnut trotted in from the kitchen, spied Fern, and meowed happily. Then Fern mellowed right down.

The kittens purred and rubbed their faces together, as if it had been ages and they were glad to see each other. Oak and Alder watched them together. It felt really good to see how happy the kittens were to see one another. And Oak was glad that she had decided to be nice that afternoon in the cafeteria.

"What's all this?" Alder said, appraising the food on the coffee table.

"The snacks I made," Oak said, and before she could stop him, Alder had reached into one of the bowls, picked up a heart-shaped tuna treat, and popped it into his mouth.

"Oh," said Oak, "those are for the kittens!"

Alder coughed and choked, but it was too late—he'd already chewed and started to swallow, and there was nowhere for the tuna treat to go but down. Oak quickly poured him some tea and handed him the cup.

Alder took a big swig of tea, swishing it around in his cheeks like mouthwash. At last, he swallowed. "Gross," he said.

"Um, yeah," said Oak. "I don't think they use human-grade tuna in cat treats. Here," she said. "Have a sandwich."

Alder sat on the couch and bit into the sandwich—a bit dubiously at first, which Oak understood, after the cat treat. Oak poured a cup of tea for herself and poured a little cream into a shallow bowl for each kitten. They were nowhere to be found, and for a moment, Oak felt certain that they'd somehow escaped again.

She went through the house, calling, "Here, kitty, kitty! Here, kitty!"

They weren't in the kitchen, nor her bedroom, and the

doors to her parents' bedroom and the office were both closed. The bathroom was empty.

"Kitties! Walnut! Fern!" Oak tried to make her voice playful and sweet, but panic set it on edge, made it dissonant.

There was a movement from Alder's backpack, where he'd shrugged it off in the entry hall. Then an orange-striped tail and rump backed out of it. Walnut! Then, shaking her way out of the bag, came Fern as well.

Oak could have melted with relief. "You bad kitties," she admonished, but her voice was light now, happy. She picked up Alder's backpack to zip it, so the cats couldn't get inside again.

There, in the shadow of the bag, was a golden glint.

Oak peeked inside. It was something rectangular, covered in cloth. She knew it wasn't polite to rummage through someone else's stuff, but even still, she reached in and pulled it out. Then she gasped.

There it was—a plain black book, slightly smaller than most books, with gilded letters in yellow gold down its spine: *Feline Teleportation*.

CHAPTER 19

The cream cheese and salmon sandwiches were quite good. Alder took another happy bite. He heard the kittens rustling around, and then they came running wildly into the living room, one long burst of orange.

Behind him, in the entry hall, Oak was fussing around with something; Alder could hear her.

"Alder," Oak said, and her voice sounded . . . different. It was soft, and very serious, as if she had seen a ghost. "Where did you get this?"

He turned around. She was standing in the doorway to the living room, holding a book—the one he'd brought to school that morning to give to her. "Oh," he said. "That's for you. To say sorry for being such a jerk the other day. I don't know." He shrugged. "It seemed to have your name on it."

Oak walked slowly into the room. She lowered herself onto the couch next to Alder. "What do you mean, it had my name on it?" She set the book on the coffee table, but her gaze did not leave its cover.

"It's just an expression," Alder said. "I know it's probably silly, like a joke book or something, but its title made me think of what happened the other day. Oak, are you okay?"

"Where did you get this?" Oak said again.

"My mom bought it last week, at the library's book sale," Alder said. "She brought it home with a bunch of other books, and she told me I could have as many of them as I wanted. And then, after what happened the other day in the cafeteria . . ." Alder cleared his throat and tried again, setting the sandwich back on the plate. "After what I did last week, when I ignored you at the table . . . well, I felt bad, and I wanted to give you something. And I saw this book, and I don't know *why*, I just felt like you should have it. Like it should be yours. So I brought it over." He paused. "You don't like it?"

Slowly, Oak blew out her breath. She reached over and poked the book, as if maybe she expected it to move.

When she looked up at him, her eyes were full wonder.

His voice came out in a whisper. "Oak," he said again. "Are you all right?"

"It barely seems possible," she said, and her voice was quiet too. "What are the odds?"

Normally, it would make Alder very cranky if he asked someone questions and they didn't get answered, but for some reason, this felt different. It felt like, when the answer came, it would be worth waiting for. And so he waited.

He didn't have to wait terribly long. No more than a few seconds, really. And then Oak blinked, as if to clear her vision, as if to bring herself back to the moment.

"Okay," she said. "Listen."

And then she told him about how she had arranged all their family books in a big rainbow on their bookshelf, with the black books in the bottom right corner, and then her mother had rearranged them (Oak actually said "disarranged," which sounded worse to Alder than "rearranged"), and how Oak had gone looking for a book later whose title she couldn't remember—"Only that it had the word *Feline* in it," she said, and that it was a gift that her father had given her mother—but she couldn't find it anywhere. Her mother, Oak said, had told her that she'd boxed up some of the books to donate to the library's book sale, and so Oak had ridden her bike all the way to the library on Saturday, only to find that she was too late, that the sale was over and the books were all gone.

"*My* mom brought this book home last week," Alder murmured. "Remember? When you were over at my house? And she came in with a stack of books from the library? That book"—Alder pointed at the book, but he didn't touch it; actually, it made him a little nervous now—"was in the stack! It was sitting in my house the whole time. While you were searching your house for it. While you were riding to the library to find it."

"All this time," said Oak, her voice reverent, "and it was right next door."

She looked up and straight at Alder. He looked straight at her. Her eyes, he noticed, were a deep dark brown.

They looked at each other for a long moment, and something like a jolt of electricity passed between them. The kittens seemed to notice, for they began meowing in unison, and they jumped up on the couch and wove back and forth between Alder and Oak, purring and headbutting, as if they felt the burst of energy and wanted to be a part of it.

"Oak," said Alder, "where did you say your dad got this book?"

"He brought it home from a business trip he took," Oak said. "He said he found it in some weird shop."

"I don't suppose . . . ," said Alder, "by any chance, was the shop in Seattle?"

"How did you know that?" Oak asked.

Alder had the strangest feeling, like he was almost afraid to ask the next question, but he did anyway. "Could it have been the Ballyhoo Curiosity Shop?"

Oak's eyes went round, and the kittens' meowing grew louder, as if they were joined in song. "Is that where . . . where your mom and dad found Mort?"

Alder simply nodded.

There was nothing else to say for a while. Oak and Alder just stared at each other, and at the book. The kittens, whose calls seemed to crescendo, began to lick each other's heads.

"I suppose sometimes weird things just happen," Alder suggested.

"Yes," said Oak. "But it seems like lots of weird things are happening to us."

"The house," said Alder, his voice dropping to a whisper. "And Mort."

Oak nodded. "And before that, the kittens."

That's right. The kittens were from the same litter, separated and then reunited here, as next-door neighbors.

"What do you think we should do?" Alder asked.

"I think," said Oak, "that we should read the book."

They turned together to look at the book. It had no dust jacket; it was matte black, cloth covered, and no taller than a hand. There were no words at all on the front or back cover, only along the spine, which read *Feline Teleportation* in gold letters that caught the light and shimmered.

Fern had curled into a ball in Alder's lap; she purred. Walnut had curled into a ball in Oak's lap; he purred, too.

Alder watched as Oak reached out for the book; she hesitated for a moment, her hand hovering above it, as if she were afraid, but then she picked it up. She settled back into the couch, and Alder settled behind her. Fern was a warm,

175

pleasant weight in his lap. He watched Oak's hands as she flipped open the book.

The first page read, simply:

FELINE TELEPORTATION
A Guide

Edith Phipps, PhD

Oak turned the page; there was a table of contents, which interested Alder, but Oak turned right past it to the next page, which read:

INTRODUCTION
A Brief History of the Art and Magic
of Feline Travel through Time and Space

Welcome, dear reader. If this book has found its way to you, consider yourself lucky. After all, who among us truly finds what we desire? Not many, I'd wager.

Now, I can practically feel your dubiousness radiating across the space-time continuum. "Teleporting cats?" you are most likely mumbling, if not aloud, then at least in your head. For these days, we like to think that we are beyond the epoch of believing in such things. But ask yourself: When was the last time you encountered something for which you could find no plausible explanation? And is it that hard to accept that, perhaps, the truest explanation is an implausible one? Implausible, after all, is not the same as impossible.

"What's 'implausible'?" Alder asked.

"Not likely to be true," Oak answered.

"Oh," said Alder, and he returned to the page.

If you doubt the veracity of this subject matter, then you are not alone. My own peers in the scientific community seem to find my research in this area to be "laughable" (their repeated words, not mine). But if today's "top" science minds cannot expand enough to consider the wonders of feline parallel universe teleportation, then perhaps, dear reader, yours can.

"That's a bunch of words I don't really understand," Alder said.

"It means that other scientists don't believe in her research about cats teleporting," said Oak. "Now shhh."

The unique ability of cats to teleport to parallel universes and hidden spaces has been known by a few discerning human beings over the past epochs. Indeed, the earliest record of this feline proclivity was made by ancient Egyptians; unfortunately, that body of research was lost when the libraries at Alexandria burned. A tragedy for a scientist such as myself, most definitely. But not such a tragedy, I'd wager, for felines; they are, after all, a secretive society, and I would not entirely dismiss the possibility that the cats themselves lit fire to the libraries in order to protect their fiercely guarded knowledge.

It is essential, therefore, that anyone who wishes to accompany cats in their teleportation must first understand the etiquette of it. The universal laws that allow for teleportation have always existed, of course; energy cannot be created or destroyed. It can only be harnessed and set free. It's the etiquette and the mechanics of teleportation, exclusively developed and refined over millennia by cats alone, that have allowed them to harness this power and to readily utilize it.

As for the most fundamental question—that is, why cats teleport in the first place—alas, there I have no definite answers. Though we cannot truly know their intentions, it does seem to me, after a lifetime of research, that cats travel with purpose, as they do everything with purpose.

Regardless of the unknowability of their intentions, there is still much I can share with you about my observations in this remarkable field of study. And, as the world's foremost—perhaps only—expert in feline teleportation, I salute your curiosity, your courage, and your much-warranted faith in the exceptional abilities of felines.

Alder had just reached the end of the introduction when Oak shut the book. She flipped it over, as if she thought that perhaps some words might appear on the back, which, of course, did not happen.

Then she turned back to the very first page, the one labeled *Feline Teleportation, A Guide,* with the author's name.

"It doesn't make any sense," Oak murmured. She flipped back and forth from the title page to the introduction, as if she were searching for a page that wasn't there.

"What doesn't make sense?" Alder asked.

"There's none of the usual stuff," Oak said. "Like, I don't know, the numbers and dates and information that's at the beginning of books."

Alder must have looked as confused as he felt, because Oak got up and grabbed another book at random from the shelf.

"Look," she said, and she flipped open the book—a novel with a picture of the ocean on the front with the title *The Waves of Memory*—to the title page. Its reverse side did have a bunch of words and numbers: it had a copyright date; it had a short disclaimer that read "All rights reserved. No part of this book may be used or reproduced in in any matter whatsoever without the written permission of the publisher." It had the name of the publisher, and a couple of long strings of numbers with the letters *ISBN* in front of them.

Feline Teleportation had none of this. Just the title page, and then the book began.

"That *is* strange," Alder agreed. But it didn't seem the strangest thing to him, not by far. "Let's read more, okay?"

Oak nodded and flipped back to the introduction, and then past it to the page labeled *Chapter One: Teleportation: A History.*

There was a noise from the hallway—a door opening.

"Oak?"

Hearing Oak's mother's voice made Alder feel nervous. He'd forgiven Oak for what had happened to the tree, and for the other things, too, like shoving him, but he remembered the tone of his own mother's voice when Oak's mom had ordered the tree to its death, the way Alder's mom had said, *That woman.*

He felt, suddenly, panicky and overwhelmed. He didn't know why *this* was the thing that disturbed him, after everything else he'd experienced in the past few days—all the strangeness, all the oddities—but suddenly, with the sound of Oak's mother's voice, it was too much, and Alder knew that he needed to go home.

"I've gotta go," he said.

"What do you mean—?" Oak began, but Alder had already wrapped one hand around Fern, and he stood, tucking her inside his cardigan. Shoving his feet into his shoes and throwing his backpack over his shoulder, he reached for the handle of Oak's front door. This door was orange, not green like his, not plain wood like the third door—Mort's door—but other than the color, this door could have been any one of those, and Alder had the strangest feeling, like anything could be on the other side.

He stood still, his hand on the silver knob, almost afraid to turn it. Then he yanked it open to a perfectly normal view of his perfectly normal street, and there was his own house next door. His perfectly normal house.

Chin tucked, kitten cradled, Alder hurried home.

CHAPTER 20

"**D**id your friend leave already?" Oak's mom asked. She was holding the mug Oak had brought her.

"He just rushed out," Oak said. Through the front window, she watched the back of Alder's dark, curly head as he hurried down her front path and then turned left up the sidewalk and disappeared from view.

"I was just going to see if you guys felt like pizza." Mom took in the leftover sandwiches and tea. "But it looks like you already ate."

"Just a snack," Oak said. And then, "Mom, the weirdest thing happened." *Feline Teleportation* was still open on her lap, along with Walnut. "Remember I was looking for a book? The one you gave away? Well, you'll never believe it—the lady right next door, our new neighbor, she actually *bought it* at the library sale, and Alder brought it over to give to me! Isn't that bizarre?"

"The neighbor?" Oak's mom said. "Which one?"

"The one on the other side of the tree," Oak answered. "The tree you cut down."

The thing about Mom's super-short hair was that there was nothing to disguise her expression—no bangs, no forward-falling locks of hair, nothing. So when her eyebrows arched and her mouth opened in surprise, and then when, a flash later, she drew her whole face closed like a shuttered window, Oak saw everything.

"You say that like I *wanted* to get rid of the tree," Mom said. "Like I enjoyed it or something. I don't just go around looking for trees to cut down, you know."

Oak didn't know what to say.

Mom's voice went higher, louder. "We needed to build another bedroom if we were all going to live here. Sometimes, a tree has to go. Sometimes, one thing has to end to make room for something else. All of us have to make hard choices, Oak. Someday, you will understand."

The wonder and magic of the book drained away, replaced by Oak's quick anger. "You're always saying that," she said, as loud as her mother, which woke up Walnut, who hopped down from her lap. Oak got up also, too mad, suddenly, to stay sitting. "You say that someday I'll understand, but *you* don't understand all kinds of things,

183

so what makes you so sure *I* will? And you know what's even harder than making hard choices? Dealing with hard choices someone else got to make."

Mom didn't say anything, but her eyebrows were up in twin surprised arches. Her forehead crinkled all across. "Is this about the move?" she said at last.

"Take your pick!" Oak said. "The move. The tree. The bookshelf."

"The bookshelf? What about the bookshelf?"

Did her mom even *remember*? "You rearranged all the books," Oak said.

"Oh, that," Mom said. "Honey, I didn't think you'd mind. It was pretty the way you did it, but I couldn't find anything."

"Well," said Oak, "I *did* mind. I mind all of it." Her throat felt thick, tight. "You could have asked me what I thought about moving."

"Oak, honey, sometimes grown-ups have to make decisions that aren't popular with kids. Like moving. Or cutting down trees. Not everything can be a vote."

"*We're not a democracy*," Oak said, quoting her mom.

"That's right," Mom said. "We are on some things, but not on all the things. But the bookshelf—you're right about that. I should have asked. We can put the books back the way you had them, if you want."

Oak shook her head. Putting the books back into a

rainbow wouldn't change anything real. Anything that mattered.

"And we can paint your room," Mom said. "Any color you want."

"Black?" Oak asked. She didn't even want a black room.

"Well," Mom said, "any color *within reason*."

That was the problem—what felt reasonable to Oak and what felt reasonable to her mother weren't the same.

"As for the tree—"

"I don't want to talk about the tree anymore," Oak said.

Her mom set the mug down on an end table and rubbed her face with both hands. "Okay," she said, but then she said, "I can't uncut the tree. I can't unmove the move." Mom's hands dropped to her sides. "This new job," she said, "is tougher than I thought. It's stressful. And the construction, all the mess and dust. And I miss your dad."

Walnut meowed and made a figure eight between Oak and her mother, purring and circling as if to knit them together, but neither of them took a step toward the other.

"I miss him too," Oak said.

"Of course you do," said her mom. She sat down on the couch. "It'll all work out. It just takes time." She patted the spot next to her, but Oak didn't sit. "Now, what was it you were saying? Something about a book?"

Just a few moments ago, Oak had been on the verge of telling her mom all about the strange book, and the kitten

185

coincidence, and maybe even about Mort. But now . . .
"Never mind," Oak said. "It's nothing."

"Nothing's *nothing*," Mom said. "Even 'nothing' is *something*. It's nothing." She smiled at the joke, but Oak refused to smile.

Still, she wanted the conversation to be over, and Oak knew that when she wanted her mom to drop a subject, the best tactic was to bring up another. "How are the blueprints coming?"

"Oh, fine," said Mom. "It's no Palace of Fine Arts."

This was a joke Mom often made when she was working on a project that wasn't particularly artistic—comparing it to her favorite San Francisco structure.

"Well, they can't all be the Palace of Fine Arts," Oak answered, which was what her father usually said in reply.

"That's right," Mom said, running her hand across her hair. "So," she said, "pizza?"

While they were waiting for the pizza to be delivered, Oak tucked the book safely and secretly away in her room, inside a pillowcase on her bed. As she did, she pictured the look on her mother's face when she had told her that the book had come from the woman next door. She had seen a similar look somewhere else lately . . . where was it?

Her gaze drifted out her bedroom window. And then she remembered—Alder's mother. The way she had looked when she'd come home to find Oak sitting in her front room. No, that wasn't exactly true; when she'd first seen Oak there, she had looked happy about it, like maybe she was glad to see that Alder had a visitor. It was only after he had told her that Oak was the new next-door neighbor that her expression had shifted.

Oak had said to Alder then, "That was weird, wasn't it?"

And now she found herself saying the same thing again, this time to herself, about her own mother: "That was weird, wasn't it?"

There was no one to answer her question except for Walnut, who had nothing to say on the matter. And, Oak ruminated, the list of things to which her question could apply—the kitten coincidence; the apparition of the house that wasn't there, and its strange inhabitant; the disappearance and reappearance of *Feline Teleportation*—all of it was weird.

But even in the midst of weirdness, most things stayed reliably commonplace. Dinner and dishes; kitty litter and showers; homework and bedtime.

Oak had just managed to get through all the things she had to do for the evening when her mom poked her head into her bedroom to say, in her regular voice, with no trace of her earlier upsetness, "Lights out, ladybird!"

"Already?" said Oak.

"Morning comes early," said Mom. She crossed the room to turn down Oak's bedcovers. Oak was seized with a sudden fear that Mom would fluff her pillow, discover the book, and take it away, which was completely irrational, because the book had been on their family's bookshelf less than a week ago. There was nothing contraband about it.

Still, the fear persisted.

Mom's hand grazed the pillow, but just then Walnut decided it was time to play, and he attacked Mom's slippered feet as if they were two great warships and he was the kraken, determined to take them down.

"Ow!" Mom yelped and turned away from the bed. "Walnut, cut it out!"

Now Walnut purred and flipped onto his back, stretching his front legs up high to expose his orange-and-cream belly. No one could resist such a sight; Mom cooed and knelt to scratch him, and Oak dove into bed, thumping her head onto her pillow and pinning the book into place.

"Good night, Mom," Oak said. "Hand me Walnut, will you?"

Mom scooped up the kitten and kissed his head before tucking him in along with Oak. "Sleep well," she said, and she turned off the light on her way out, leaving Oak's door cracked open.

She would wait until Mom's light went off. And then

she'd get a flashlight from the kitchen, and she'd fish the book out from her pillowcase, and she'd see what *Feline Teleportation* was all about.

It was a good plan. A solid plan. But as Walnut purred and knit his paws into Oak's arm, as he rubbed his head beneath her chin and settled warmly into sleep, Oak's eyes grew heavy too, and she felt her thoughts slip away on the vibrations of his purrs.

I'll just close my eyes for a few minutes, she thought.

"Oak!"

Oak's eyes shot open, then squeezed shut at the sudden assault of light.

"Honey, we overslept," called Mom.

Oak groaned, and against her side, Walnut echoed her protest with a weak *mew.* She heard the sound of Mom pushing Oak's bedroom door all the way open. "Up and at 'em," Mom said.

Oak could feel her mother standing in the doorway, and she knew she wouldn't leave until she saw, as she liked to say, "the whites" of Oak's eyes.

With great reluctance, Oak peeled her eyes open. "I'm up," she croaked.

"You may be marginally awake, but you aren't yet up," Mom said.

She was too tired to argue, so Oak chose the path of

least resistance and threw back the covers, swinging her legs over the edge of her bed. Startled by the movement, Walnut shot off, racing past Mom and away into the house.

"I'm up," Oak said again, and this time, Mom nodded in agreement.

"The bus will be here in fifteen minutes," she said. "I'll make you some toast for the road."

"Road toast," mumbled Oak.

"Fifteen minutes!" Mom called from the kitchen.

Oak rubbed her eyes, sighed, and began to get ready for the day.

Toast in hand, hair unbrushed, Oak barely made it to the bus in time.

In fact, she didn't quite. "Wait!" she yelled as it began to pull away, but there was no way Faith could hear her through the thick glass doors, over the rumble of the engine.

But then the bus stopped anyway, just a few feet down the road, and the doors hissed open, and Faith called out, "Hiya, tree girl! Tree boy told me to stop."

And there was Alder, smiling a small smile halfway down the bus on the street side. "I saved you a seat," he said, "and I watched out the window just in case you were coming after all."

"Thanks," said Oak. "I overslept." She offered Alder a slice of toast.

"Thanks," he said, and they fell into companionable silence as they ate.

The bus turned out of their neighborhood and onto the main street. Sitting comfortably next to Alder, Oak remembered the way she had felt about him not that long ago, on the day she'd been so angry and frustrated that she'd shoved him out of her way. She remembered the satisfaction of watching him fall.

"Alder," she said.

"Mm-hm," he answered, taking another bite of the toast.

"I never really apologized for that time."

"What time?"

"That time I pushed you down. I'm really sorry. That was mean. I promise I'll never do it again."

Alder looked over at Oak and smiled. "That's all right," he said. "I forgive you."

"Thank you," said Oak. There was a lump in her throat that was not peanut butter toast.

"Let's be friends," Alder said suddenly, and he looked a bit startled, as if he didn't know he was going to say those words until after he had said them.

Oak swallowed. "Okay," she said.

And it was almost magic, or maybe there was no "almost" about it. Those words, said, felt like a charm.

When the bus arrived at school and Faith called out, "Bye, tree kids," Oak and Alder answered in unison.

"Bye, Faith!" they said. And, tree kids together, they went inside.

CHAPTER 21

At lunch, Alder did have a brief flash of hope that maybe Cynthia would have forgotten her mom's knitting stuff. She had not.

In fact, by the time Alder had made his way over to the girls' lunch table, Cynthia had taken everything out of her bag: five sets of needles, ranging from thick to thin, and a half dozen skeins of yarn in various sizes and thicknesses. And Cameron had her sweater, the red one with the hole in the arm near the elbow. They were really going to do this, then.

"Okay," said Alder by way of greeting. "One thing at a time. Repairing a sweater is a whole different thing than starting a new knitting project. What should we do first?"

"Let's fix Cameron's sweater," said Oak, "since that's what got us started down this road in the first place."

Alder appraised the thickness of the yarn in Cameron's sweater. It was medium, probably wool, and tomato red.

There was no perfect match among the yarn selections Cynthia had brought; in fact, none of the skeins were even close. Alder unzipped his backpack.

"I brought some yarn from home," he said. "It's probably not exactly right, but I thought it would be better than nothing . . ." He extracted a small paper bag from the bottom of his backpack and turned it upside down. A ball of dark-red yarn spilled out. It was more burgundy than tomato, but the thickness was almost perfectly matched.

"Hey!" said, Cameron, pleased. "That's great!"

From the smaller pocket of his backpack, Alder fished out a little leather pouch that held a set of oversize sewing needles. "Fixing a hole," he explained, "is really more about sewing than knitting. It's actually called darning." He wet the end of the yarn in his mouth, then lined it up with the eye of the needle. He felt a little flutter of pride when it went through on the very first try. "Knitting is really just a series of fancy knots," he went on, "but darning is more about weaving back and forth."

He set aside the yarn and the needle and picked up Cameron's sweater. He pulled the sleeve inside out.

"Oak," he said, "can I borrow your water bottle?"

She had one of the cylindrical metal reusable bottles, which she passed to him. Alder made sure the lid was on tight and then put it in the sweater sleeve to brace it.

"Okay," he said, "here we go."

The hole was the size of a quarter. Alder made his first stitch about half an inch to the left of it. "You want to leave a tail," he said, indicating the extra yarn he had left hanging, "so that you have something to tie off with at the end."

He looked up. All of them—Oak and Cynthia, Miriam and Cameron and Carmen—were watching as if he were doing something really cool instead of just darning up an old sweater.

He cleared his throat. "Then you just pick up every other stitch, like this." He wove the needle over one stitch, under the next, and over the one after that, then pulled the yarn through. "What I'm doing is starting to make a sort of an anchor, for when I go over the hole." He stitched about a two-inch line, then wove back in the other direction. "When you get to the hole," he said, "you just stretch the yarn straight across it, like this, and then pick up your stitches again."

He went on like that, back and forth, and then did a few more rows on the other side, to anchor it down again. "Then you've got to do the same thing in the other direction," he said as he worked, "except this time, when you get to the hole, you weave over and under the new stitches across the hole, just like you do with the other stitches, see?"

Someone—one of the twins, maybe, gasped a little when the weaving across the hole was complete.

"It's not perfect," Alder admitted. "The color is a little off, and you can see where the new stitches are, but it's better than a hole. And the repair will keep it from getting worse." He tied off each tail of the yarn and took a small pair of silver scissors from his leather pouch, snipping off the remainders.

Then he extracted Oak's water bottle and turned the sleeve right side out. "And, voilà!" he said, grinning and feeling sort of shy. "Not quite as good as new, but better than before."

All the girls clapped, and Cameron took back her sweater and clutched it close. "Alder, thank you," she said.

"Now," said Oak, "show us how to make fancy knots."

By the time the bell rang, each of the girls had the beginning a very short, skinny scarf.

"Not bad, not bad," Alder said as they packed up their yarn and needles.

"Let's bring our scarves back tomorrow," Cynthia suggested, and everyone nodded.

Alder walked to class and slid into his seat with a warm, full feeling in his chest.

"So, you knit?"

Alder looked up. It was Beck, looming over him. The

warm, full feeling turned to a block of ice.

"Um," said Alder.

"I saw you knitting in the cafeteria," Beck said.

Alder wasn't quite sure how to respond. Why had Beck asked him if he knit if he already knew the answer? Actually, why had Beck asked him if he could knit *at all*? Alder hadn't ever seen Beck acting mean to anyone, but in Alder's experience with Marcus, being a knitter was a pretty solid reason to get teased.

"What does it matter if I knit?" Alder asked. He folded his arms and did his best to look tough. As he did, he considered if the fact that he was defending a knitting hobby was undercutting his toughness.

Beck put his hands on Alder's desk and leaned forward, about to say something, but then Mr. Rivera said, "All right, everyone, settle down and take your seats. We need to get started."

Never had Alder been so relieved to hear the royal *we*.

"Wait for me after school, okay?" Beck said, and he rapped his knuckles on Alder's desk.

When the final bell rang three hours later, Alder was out of his seat and down the hallway like a shot. He didn't wait for Beck; he didn't wait for anyone. And for the first time all year, Alder was glad that there was such a thing as cross-country club. It meant that Marcus wouldn't be on the bus, but it meant that Beck wouldn't be either.

He was the first kid aboard, and he saved a seat for Oak, who slid comfortably beside him.

"What was *that* about?" she asked. "I've never seen you move so fast."

"Beck wanted to talk to me about knitting," Alder said, "and I didn't much feel like having that conversation."

Oak laughed. "Maybe he wanted to compare techniques."

Alder had no idea what Beck wanted. But the idea of talking about knitting with the coolest boy in fifth grade didn't sound like fun. It sounded humiliating.

But he didn't need to think about that now. Alder was on the bus and Beck wasn't. With a sigh, Alder relaxed back into his seat. It was a pleasant ride home; the sky was full of big white puffy clouds, and there was that autumnal, crisp feeling in the air that promised leaf piles and jack-o'-lanterns soon.

"When we get home," Alder said, "let's take another look at that book."

"Exactly what I was thinking," Oak replied. Then she hesitated. "Will your mother be home, do you think?"

"Not until five," Alder answered. "She's running errands today."

"Then let's meet at your house," said Oak. "My mom . . . will be working from home."

"And you don't want us to disturb her?"

"Sort of," said Oak slowly. "Actually . . . remember how your mom was weird the other day, when I was over at your house?"

"Yeah," said Alder. He felt kind of embarrassed. "I'm sorry about that."

Oak shook her head. "Don't worry about it," she said, "because yesterday, after you left, and I told my mom who you were—that you're our next-door neighbor—*my* mom was weird, too!"

"Huh," said Alder. "Are you sure?"

"Positive," Oak said, and Alder believed her. "I think there's something strange happening with our mothers."

"Like what?"

"I don't know," Oak said, and she looked off into the middle distance, like she was trying to see something that was almost there but not quite. Then she snapped back into the present and looked Alder straight in the eye. "But I think we should find out."

Alder waited outside Oak's door as she made a brief stop inside to gather up the book and her kitten. As he waited, he looked up at the construction, at the progress being made. He could hear the workmen hammering, and the high-pitched whine of an electric saw. There was the smell of wood shavings in the air.

Then his gaze drifted to the stump, and, out of habit,

he let his eyes roam loosely around the air just above it. He hadn't seen the shimmery patch since the Sunday after he and Oak had lost their kittens and found themselves with the walking, talking Mort, but he hadn't given up the possibility of its reappearing.

Today, he thought he saw it—a shimmery glint—just for an instant. But then he made the mistake of trying to stare right at it, to catch it with his eyes as a fishing hook snags a fish, and it slipped away, as if it were too clever to be caught. When he tried to soften his gaze to see it again, it was gone.

Oak emerged from her house, Walnut tucked under one arm, the book tucked under the other. "Okay," she said.

They walked the short distance to Alder's house. He pulled out his key from his backpack and wriggled it into the lock. When the door swung open, there was Fern sitting in the front hallway, her tail wrapped neatly around her paws, as if she were waiting for them.

The kittens mewed their greeting to one another. Oak set Walnut down, and the two kittens rubbed noses, and then Fern led the way into the kitchen. *Probably sharing her kibble with her brother*, Alder imagined, and he felt proud about what a good host she was.

"Oh," he said, following Fern's example, "would you like something to drink?"

"Sure," said Oak, shrugging out of her coat.

200

Alder fixed two glasses of chocolate milk and returned to the front room, where he had left Oak, but she wasn't there.

"In here," she called from the dining room.

She was standing in front of the record player, thumbing through the records. "Do you mind if we listen to some music?" she asked.

Alder set the glasses of chocolate milk on the table. "Okay," he said.

Oak pulled out the same album she'd chosen last time. "Alder," she said, "we're friends, right?"

"Yes," said Alder.

"Friends shouldn't have secrets," Oak said, "and they should help each other when they're sad." She flipped the record sleeve over. There was the photo of Alder's dad, strumming his banjo.

Alder cleared his throat. "That's my dad," he said. It felt weird to say it out loud, even though it wasn't a secret.

"That's what I figured," Oak said. She looked down at the picture, then up at Alder. "You look like him."

"You think so?" said Alder, pleased.

"Yes," said Oak, looking back and forth between the picture and Alder, then up at the family portrait on the wall. "You have his hair and his smile. You don't have his eyes, though. His are green."

"*Were* green," Alder corrected.

"*Were* green." Oak nodded. "That's true. And I'm sorry."

"Thanks," said Alder. "Me too."

It could have been uncomfortable or terribly sad, but it wasn't. It was sad, but not so sad that Alder couldn't handle it. And it wasn't uncomfortable. It was oddly *comfortable*, actually, to talk about his dad with Oak. It felt nice. "Do you want to hear my favorite of his songs?" Alder offered.

"Yes," said Oak.

Alder knelt in front of the record collection and flipped through them until he found the one he was looking for.

"Here it is," he said. It was from his father's final album. There was no photo of him on this jacket; Alder didn't know why.

The name of the album was *Fly, Bird, Fly.*

"This is the only album he made after I was born," Alder told Oak as he pulled the record from its sleeve and set it gently on the turntable. He pressed the switch to start the record spinning. The arm lifted from its place and rotated, then dropped its needle onto the vinyl. There was a moment of scritch-scratch, and then the song began.

Little bluebird, baby guy
Sweetest bird in the big blue sky
One day you'll spread your wings and fly
Don't know when, but I know why
That's what birdies do—they fly.

Bluebird boy, my sweet hatchling
Truest rhyme I'll ever bring
Sweetest song I'll ever sing
I'll fly too when you spread those wings
That's what birdies do—they sing.

Don't know how, my bluebird boy
Don't know why, my bluebird joy
Don't know where, my bluebird true
All I know is I love you
That's all this Canary bird can do—
I
Love
You.

CHAPTER 22

"That was beautiful," Oak said, and she wiped tears from her cheeks. The song made her miss her own dad. She missed the way he called her "kiddo." She missed the smell of his deodorant. She missed the way he made her laugh, and Mom too. Suddenly, she didn't know how she could be apart from him for even one more month. It seemed impossibly long but, of course, this wasn't something she would say to Alder, who would never see his dad again.

"He really loved you," she said instead.

Alder nodded. "I wish I remembered more about him." Carefully, he removed the record from the turntable and slipped it back into its sleeve. "I'm glad I have his music," he said. "But I wish I had more." Then he chose another album, this one just instruments with no lyrics. Oak could hear a piano and a guitar and some sort of horn, a saxophone maybe. It was soft background music that felt sort of like texture.

Oak picked up her chocolate milk and *Feline Teleportation* from where she'd set it on the table and said, "Want to read it with me?"

Alder nodded and followed Oak back into the front room. They fell together onto the couch.

Oak held the book on her lap, but she angled it so they could both see the pages clearly. She flipped past the title page to the next page, which read:

TABLE OF CONTENTS

They had already read the introduction; the first chapter said it was a longer history of cat teleportation, but also that it could be skipped in a hurry.

"Are we in a hurry?" Oak asked Alder.

"I'm not," he said, so Oak turned to *Chapter One: A Longer History.*

> *It may surprise you to learn that as long as the feline has cohabited with humans, it has been keeping a secret from us . . . or most of us. Most people don't pay good enough attention to notice when their feline companion has slipped away. Most people, dear reader, don't notice most things, feline-related or otherwise.*
>
> *Most cat owners, upon noticing their cat has*

gone missing (if they notice at all), assume that the tabby has simply popped over the wall to visit the neighbors' garden, or that their polydactyl Siamese must be napping in the back of a closet. And then they scoff at how much their kitty sleeps, calling their feline "lazy" or some such nonsense, because they never know about the tremendous expenditure of energy it takes for a cat to leap through unseen windows into the secret pockets of our world. Imagine! They call their cats lethargic loafers, when the truth is that their cat has potentially conducted a full day of interdimensional travel, visiting locations their owner could never dream of, while the human couldn't even be bothered to rinse out the cereal bowl.

Paying attention, dear reader, is the key to most things. And one young man can serve as a prime example of what happens when you pay attention . . . especially to your cat.

Perhaps you've heard of Nikola Tesla, engineer and inventor of the first electric alternating-current motor? If not, that is not the fault of his cat. Even the finest feline cannot teach its human the art of business savvy, and that is why these days you pay your electric bill to Consolidated Edison, Inc., rather than Consolidated Tesla, Inc.

Still, young Nikola Tesla's cat did his best. Nikola's marvelous Macak might truly be called the father of electricity, as it was due to this feline that Nikola became enamored of electricity's spark. About Macak, Nikola once wrote,

"I wish I could give you an adequate idea of the affection that existed between us. We lived for one another. Wherever I went, Macak followed, because of our mutual love and his desire to protect me. When such a necessity presented itself, he would rise to twice his normal height, buckle his back, and with his tail as rigid as a metal bar and whiskers like steel wires, he would give vent to his rage with explosive puffs: Pfftt! Pfftt! It was a terrifying sight, and whoever had provoked him, human or animal, would beat a hasty retreat."

And it was Macak himself who introduced young Nikola to electricity! One night, as Nikola petted his cat, something amazing happened. Nikola told the story as follows:

"In the dusk of the evening, as I stroked Macak's back, I saw a miracle that made me speechless with amazement. Macak's back was a sheet of *light and my hand produced a shower of sparks loud enough to be heard all over the house."*

Yes! That stroke of static electricity was the spark of all that followed for young Nikola, who spent the remainder of his life chasing the magic of electricity, aided by Macak, as long as he was able.

What Nikola's letters don't include are the many lessons in portal travel he gained from Macak. We will get into those lessons in later chapters, but suffice it to say that Macak was a first-rate feline teleporter in his younger days.

"Static electricity," said Alder, "is that, like, when you get a shock?"

Oak nodded. "It has to do with things rubbing together, and dry air, I think." But, she realized, she didn't really know much more than that. She made a mental note to learn more about how static electricity worked, and then she turned her attention back to *Feline Teleportation*.

After the section about Tesla and Macak, the author went on to talk about a whole slate of other historical cats who traveled through portals, and they all shared an important thing in common: each story had something to do with electricity.

The end of the chapter read:

Now, maybe you're wondering: Why doesn't everyone know about the teleporting abilities of felines?

Well, dear reader, not all cats possess the same abilities, and not all humans possess the wits to notice. There are even those among us (and among my esteemed cohort of scientists) who choose to be obtuse when it comes to the miraculous. And, of the cats who teleport, it's one in a million who decides to share its secret with its human . . . and maybe even fewer than that.

Might you, at this very moment, be in possession of a teleporting feline? There are some ways to tell. Turn to the next chapter to learn more.

"This is the weirdest book I've ever read," Alder said. "Do you think any of it is real?"

"I hope all of it is real," said Oak. "Let's check." She set down the book. "Do you have a computer?"

Alder went to get his laptop from his room. While she waited, Oak got up and poked around, looking for the kittens. At first, she couldn't find them, and she wondered if it was possible that maybe they were gone. Teleporting.

But then she found them lumped together on top of one of the afghan blankets, in a basket in Alder's dining room. Asleep, they were almost indistinguishable, fuzzy arms and legs entwined. Were they dreaming, perhaps about portals and oversize opossums? Oak wished she could teleport into their minds to find out.

"Hey," called Alder, who had the computer. Oak returned to the couch and watched as he typed "Nikola Tesla and his cat" into his browser. She read over his shoulder as he scrolled through the first article that popped up.

"It *is* true," Alder said, his voice almost reverent. He looked up at Oak. "Do you think—if the electricity stuff is true—that *all* of it is true?"

"Well," Oak pointed out, "there's nothing on your computer about Tesla's cat teaching him about portal travel. But . . . we know that part is true already, don't we? Because of Mort? The cats escaped from our houses and made their way into his somehow."

Alder nodded.

"So, then," said Oak.

"Maybe," said Alder.

Neither of them had drunk the chocolate milk. Each picked up their glass and sank back into the couch, lost in thought.

"I think," said Oak, "that our kittens opened the portal. And—maybe this is where Tesla comes in!—I think it's because of the *lightning* that we were pulled in after."

Alder nodded slowly. "I was thinking the same thing."

"And the portal is by the tree stump," said Oak. "I've seen something there."

Alder sat up straight. "Like, a shimmer? Like a patch of shiny air?"

"Yes! You've seen it?" Even after all the things they'd seen—all the coincidences, all the strangeness—Oak felt relieved to learn that Alder had seen the shimmer, too.

"Uh-huh," said Alder. "A few times. But whenever I try to look right at it, it disappears."

"Like you can only see it from the side. Or when you're not really focusing on it."

"Exactly!" Alder sounded pleased to hear that Oak shared his experience too. Then, "We're lucky we made it back all right. That we weren't hurt or anything."

"Uh-huh," said Oak. "And we're even luckier that we got to go!" She remembered the wooden door, the strange creature, his little boots. "I want to go back," she said.

"Oh," said Alder. "I don't know if that's a very good idea."

"Why not?"

"Because," said Alder, "aren't you scared?"

"Maybe," Oak admitted. "A little. But in a good way. I feel like . . . well, we must have ended up there for a reason, don't you think? It's your opossum that lives there, after all! We just have to figure out how to get there." She tapped the book.

As if on cue, the kittens rose from their slumber and padded into the front room. Walnut jumped on the coffee table, sat down, and licked his paw prettily, using it to smooth his whiskers. Fern hopped onto Oak's lap and yawned, her pink barbed tongue arching out from between sharp white fangs.

"My mom will be home soon," Alder said.

Oak nodded. "I'd better get home anyway. Mom's making split pea soup for dinner."

"That's my favorite," said Alder.

"Mine too. If you want, I can bring you a thermos-full for lunch tomorrow."

"Really?" Alder sounded pleased. "In that case, I'll bring an extra dessert for you."

"Okay!" said Oak. "Anything with chocolate." She passed Fern to Alder and stood, collecting her kitten and *Feline Teleportation*.

"Let me know what else you find out from the book," Alder said.

Oak nodded. She was halfway to the door when she turned and stopped. "Hey, Alder," she said, "what do you think is up with our moms?"

Alder shrugged. "I know my mom is mad about the tree. I was, too. But . . . it's not like her to hold a grudge.

My mom—well, no offense, but she usually likes *everyone*. And she really doesn't seem to like your mom at all."

Oak was not offended. "I wonder why," she said, as much to herself as to Alder.

It was another mystery—and Oak intended to solve it.

CHAPTER 23

When they climbed aboard the bus the next morning, Alder was relieved to find an empty bench near the front and, as he slipped into the window seat to make room for Oak, he pretended not to notice Beck in the back, waving to get his attention.

As soon as they were seated, even before the bus pulled away from the curb, Alder was assaulted by a rapid-fire string of information that Oak had gleaned from her midnight reading of *Feline Teleportation*.

"Did you know," she said, "that cats with four white socks can't teleport?"

Of course he didn't; he hadn't read the book. But he just grinned and shook his head.

"Did you know that cats knead because they are pressing

the fabric of the world, searching for pockets?"

He didn't.

"And cats purr to charge their motors, to rev themselves up for teleportation; did you know that? The book says that if you want to help them charge, pet them a lot."

Alder nodded and wiped the sleep dust from his eyes; actually, he hadn't slept well, due to Fern's kneading on his head and her incessant purring, nearly as loud as a truck's engine, it had seemed.

"Do you ever hear a high, ringing sound?" Oak asked.

"Sometimes," Alder answered.

"That sound is the residual effect of a cat teleporting in the vicinity," Oak said wisely.

"Ah," said Alder.

"You know that little flap, that funny thing on a cat's ear?"

Alder did.

"It's called a Henry's pocket. Do you know why?"

Alder did not.

"It's named for a cat named Henry, a cat that belonged to Henrietta Swan Leavitt. She named him after herself! Have you heard of her?"

Alder shook his head. He was trying to keep up, but it was difficult.

"Well," said Oak, and Alder settled back against the bus's vinyl bench, grateful that Oak was about to launch into something that would spare him the burden of having to respond, at least for a minute or two. "Henrietta Swan Leavitt was an American astronomer. She's mostly known for her work on luminosity—that's how bright something is—and how you can use it to measure how far away a star is. But she studied interstellar portals, too, with the help of her cat, Henry. And Henrietta lost her hearing, which makes it even stranger that the little pocket on a cat's ear is named after her and her cat, don't you think?"

Alder couldn't resist. "What's the pocket for?" he asked.

"The Henry's pocket, Henrietta Swan Leavitt discovered, is used by cats to store residual energy to help them make the return trip home through particularly challenging portals. And get this—Henrietta's cat, Henry, lived for twenty-one years, and he was able to teleport all that time! Most cats," Oak concluded, a bit know-it-all-y, Alder thought, "can only teleport during their kittenhood. And some kittens reach the end of their teleporting season at a younger age than others."

The bus was pulling into the school parking lot, and all around, kids were beginning to shoulder their backpacks. It might not be such a bad thing when the kittens couldn't teleport anymore, Alder thought. He knew Oak was keen to travel back to Mort, but Alder preferred staying in the here and now. It was more . . . predictable. Safer. "So, we don't really know how much longer Fern and Walnut will be able to teleport."

"Exactly," Oak hissed in unison with the bus's hissing door. They had arrived. "Time is of the essence."

Time, Alder said to himself, was of the essence. He nudged Oak to stand up. He wanted to get off the bus before Beck made his way down the aisle.

"See ya, tree kids," called Faith.

Alder answered, in unison with Oak, "See ya."

His brain was full of Tesla and Henrietta and Macak and Henry and Henry's pockets and pockets of other worlds, and his house and Oak's house and the house between, the house that wasn't there. His brain was so full that he didn't notice that his shoelace was untied until he tripped over it, just inside the school's front doors.

"I'll see you in class," Alder told Oak, bending to tie his shoe.

When he stood, it was to find Marcus staring at him.

"Hey," said Marcus.

"Oh," said Alder, hotly blushing. "Sorry." He didn't know why he said "sorry."

"Hey," said Marcus again, "are you avoiding Beck?"

"What?" said Alder. "No," he lied.

"Beck thinks you're avoiding him," Marcus said, scratching his nose. "He waved to you on the bus and it was like you didn't even see him."

Alder shrugged. "I guess I *didn't* see him."

"Okay," said Marcus. "Well, he wants to talk to you."

"What about?" Alder asked. His voice caught in the middle, squeaking a little.

Marcus shrugged. "He said something about knitting?"

"Uh-huh," said Alder. "Well, I'll go find him." He headed off down the hall.

"He's in the bathroom," Marcus called after him, but Alder pretended not to hear, and he went toward Mr. Rivera's class instead.

In the classroom, Alder dumped his backpack next to his desk and sank into it, miserable. If it were anyone other than *Beck*, Alder would be curious why he wanted to talk about knitting. But, if he was being totally honest with himself, Alder was intimidated by Beck. Everything seemed so easy for him: Making the teacher laugh. Running. Friend stuff.

The rest of the class began to trickle in, and then Mr. Rivera arrived, carrying his ceramic coffee mug and whistling something happy. The bell rang and the rest of the students flooded into their seats, Beck and Marcus among them. Alder felt Beck's gaze on him, pulling him like a magnet, but he forced his eyes to stay on his own desk.

"Okay, friends," Mr. Rivera said. "We're going to start off our day with interdisciplinary work. Three fifteen-minute rounds, so everyone gets with their partners. I've made a schedule for today here. . . ." He tapped on his computer keyboard, and the schedule appeared over the projector.

"I'll set a timer. Ready, friends? Find your first partner and make some noise."

Alder saw from the list that he was supposed to meet with Marcus, then Oak, then Beck.

When he got to Marcus's desk, he found Marcus had already pulled out their shared notebook. *Toenails* had been written across the cover, but Alder saw that Marcus had added the words *Fingernails and* above *Toenails.*

"I asked Mr. Rivera for permission," Marcus explained. "I figured it would give us more to write about."

"Good idea," said Alder.

Marcus grinned and flipped the notebook open to the list of subjects:

Language Arts
History
Current Events
PE
Math
Art
Science

So far, they'd filled out current events (the longest toenail lady), science (onychomycosis, a fungal infection of the toenail), math (it turned out that the World Nail

Competition judged the best nails based on a mathematical concept called the golden ratio), and PE (a list of all the physical activities that could lead to ingrown toenails).

That left art, language arts, and history.

"I took care of history," said Marcus. "I researched the nail clipper."

"You did?" Alder was impressed. It had never occurred to him to think about nail *tools*.

"Yeah," said Marcus, pulling a sheet of notes from his backpack. "The first clipper was invented by two guys . . . Eugene Heim and Oelestin Matz, in 1881."

Alder wasn't sure that Marcus was pronouncing the names right, but he didn't say this. Instead, he copied the information into the notebook and asked, "How did people cut their nails before that?"

"With a knife," Marcus said. "If I had to cut my nails with a knife, I doubt I'd have any fingers left."

Alder laughed. "Remember that time you tried to slice up a peach and ended up in the emergency room?"

Marcus held out his pointer finger. "I still have the scar."

"I've done some research, too," Alder said, reaching into his bag. "For language arts."

"Oh yeah?" said Marcus. "What did you find?"

"Well, I'm glad you checked with Mr. Rivera, because I'm pretty sure it's about fingernails, not toenails, even though it just says 'nails.' It's an old poem I found," Alder said.

"Let's hear it," said Marcus.

Alder cleared his throat, and then read:

Cut your nails on Monday, cut them for news;
Cut them on Tuesday, a new pair of shoes;
Cut them on Wednesday, cut them for health;
Cut them on Thursday, cut them for wealth;
Cut them on Friday, cut them for woe;
Cut them on Saturday, a journey you'll go;
Cut them on Sunday, you'll cut them for evil;
For all the next week you'll be ruled by the devil.

For a moment, Marcus just stared at him openmouthed. And then he started to laugh—a big, friendly guffaw. Oh, Alder had missed that laugh so much that the sound of it, and the knowledge that he'd been the one to create it, made his eyes sting with unshed tears.

"That's the craziest thing I've ever heard," Marcus said at last. "If you cut your nails on a Sunday, the devil is in charge for the whole next week?"

"I guess so," said Alder, and his smile felt so wide that he thought his face might crack open. "Which day would you cut your nails?"

"Let me see that," Marcus said, and Alder scooted his chair around to the other side of the desk so he and Marcus were shoulder to shoulder and they could read the poem together.

"Definitely not Sunday," Marcus said, "or Monday or Tuesday. Who cares about news and shoes?"

Alder nodded in agreement. "And not Friday," he said.

"What's 'woe'?" Marcus asked.

"Like, sadness, I think." Alder didn't know why he was pretending to be unsure about the meaning of "woe." He knew exactly what it meant.

"Well, I'm already healthy," said Marcus, "so not Wednesday either."

"That leaves Thursday or Saturday," Alder said. "Would you rather be rich or travel?"

"Definitely travel," Marcus said. "See the world. How about you?"

Alder thought of the kittens, and the shimmer, and the house that wasn't there. "Thursday," he answered. "I sort of like it right here."

Mr. Rivera's alarm sounded loudly. "All right, kiddos," he called. "Time to switch."

Alder stood reluctantly. "Well," he said, "I guess I'll see you later."

But Marcus had already turned his attention to his next partner, and after a moment, Alder drifted away.

Oak waited for him at her desk, their "Family" file in front of her. They had most of it filled out:

Language Arts: The Godfather (book) about crime
    families

History: Romanov family, killed July 16, 1918

Current Events: Family separations and border camps on the United States' southern border

PE: Research about benefits of family exercise

Math: "Fact families," math facts that use the same numbers

Art:

Science: DNA spit tests to learn about our families

"So, did you buy a spit test?" Oak asked, looking over the list.

"Uh-huh," said Alder. "Over the weekend. I mailed it in. I didn't understand half the questions on the form, so I just checked all the boxes."

"Me too," said Oak.

Alder craned his neck to see the list. "That just leaves art."

"I'll research an artist who specialized in family portraits," Oak said. "Easy."

Alder nodded. He looked over his shoulder at Beck, who was working with Cynthia on their project. "Say, Oak," he said, "can I ask you a question?"

Oak put down her pencil. "Sure," she said.

"It's just—" said Alder. He rubbed his neck. "Beck wants to talk to me about knitting. And I'm . . . I don't know. I guess I'm nervous?"

"What about?" Oak asked.

Alder shrugged. "What if he's going to tease me about it?"

"If he was going to tease you about it, he probably already would have," Oak said. "And anyway, who cares if he *does* tease you?"

"You know," said Alder, "last year, Marcus and I . . . hung out a lot. And this year, he's hanging out with Beck all the time."

"Oh," said Oak. "You feel like Beck stole your friend."

When he heard Oak say it, Alder knew it was ridiculous. A friend wasn't something you could *steal*, like a watch or something. But still. That was how it felt. He nodded.

"Well, *we're* friends now. And I like that you know how to knit."

"Thanks." Alder felt better, a little.

"Hey," said Oak, changing the subject, "back to what we were talking about on the bus. The kittens. And Mort. There has to be a reason, don't you think, that all that happened? We need to go back and find out more."

"I don't know," Alder said slowly. He knew how much Oak wanted to try to get back to the strange house. And he really didn't want to disappoint her. Especially now that they were friends. "Do you think it's even *safe*?" Alder asked.

"We were fine last time," Oak said.

"Yeah, but maybe we just got lucky."

"It's like Edith Phipps said in the book's introduction." Oak's voice dropped to a near whisper, forcing Alder to lean in to hear her. *"Who among us truly finds what we desire?* If we're lucky enough to have the book *and* kittens who can . . . *you know* . . . then we're practically *obligated* to try to go back to Mort's house!"

"Anyway," said Alder, reluctant to even explore the idea, "how would we get there?"

"Well," said Oak eagerly, "I've been reading the book, and—"

Just then Mr. Rivera's voice sounded again. "Okay, party people!" he called. "Rotate one more time."

"We'll talk later," Oak said. "After school."

Alder nodded. He gathered his stuff and stood. His stomach was a pit of dread.

But when he got to Beck's desk, Beck smiled with an open face. He didn't *look* like someone who wanted to tease Alder.

Slowly, Alder sat. "Hey," he said.

"Hey," said Beck. "I've been wanting to talk to you. About knitting."

Alder nodded. "I know. What's up?" He couldn't help but feel nervous, even though Beck leaned forward eagerly.

"It's just—see, my grandma was knitting me a sweater." Beck unzipped his backpack; inside, Alder could see a bright blue cable-knit sleeve. "But she died before she could finish it. And I was wondering—do you think you could finish it for me?"

Alder blinked. "Oh," he said. And then, "I'm sorry your grandmother died."

"Thanks," said Beck. His voice was gruff. "I don't even like wearing sweaters. They're itchy and hot. But . . . I'd wear this one, if I could."

Alder nodded. "Let me see it."

Beck pulled out the sweater, in pieces. Most of it was finished—the front piece, the back piece, and one sleeve. All Alder would have to do would be knit one more sleeve and then assemble the pieces. It would be easy.

"Do you have any more of this blue yarn?" Alder asked.

Beck shook his head. "The rest of Grammy's knitting stuff all got sold or taken to a thrift store."

"That's okay," said Alder. "I'll bet we've got something pretty similar at home."

"Dude," said Beck, "if you could finish it for me, I'd seriously owe you one."

Alder carefully folded up the sweater pieces and tucked them into his backpack. Maybe Beck didn't exactly "steal" Marcus. If Alder were Marcus, he'd probably prefer hanging out with Beck too. He was as nice as he was funny, and athletic, and popular. Alder zipped his backpack. "I know what it's like to miss someone," he said, and he was as careful with his words as he was with the sweater. "You don't owe me anything. I'm glad to help."

CHAPTER 24

The next two weeks were a busy time at Oak's house: the construction workers finished the addition; Oak and her mom went shopping for window coverings and new furniture for the upstairs; Oak read *Feline Teleportation* cover to cover and then began reading it again from the first page.

Oak was fascinated by the compilation of stories about teleporting cats. According to Edith Phipps, PhD, it was usually children who noticed unusual feline activity. There was one story about a tortoiseshell cat in England who disappeared and reappeared in her family's garden; the children insisted that she traveled through a portal, but their parents never believed them. And there were at least a dozen reports of cats staring off into the distance blankly, as if they were looking into a world their owners couldn't see, and many examples of cats disappearing for months at a time and then reappearing, as if by magic, none the worse for the wear.

And Edith Phipps, PhD, had a strong opinion about Schrödinger's cat. "Probably one of the most famous misunderstandings of scientific theories is that of Schrödinger's cat," she wrote near the end of chapter 1. "It's a frequent misinterpretation of his theory that a cat in a box could be considered to be simultaneously alive and dead until the box is opened; his original notes include the words 'here and not here,' which can be understood to mean both in this dimension and absent, gone through a portal. Since scientists abhor that which they cannot prove, they overwhelmingly favor the 'alive and not alive' translation to the 'here and not here' interpretation of Schrödinger's thought experiment."

Oak had never even heard of Erwin Schrödinger before she read about him and his cat in *Feline Teleportation*, so this reference led her down an interesting rabbit hole of research into quantum physics. The world, it seemed, was full of things Oak knew nothing about.

Of course, she'd known that she didn't know lots of stuff; after all, she was only eleven. How much could she have learned in just over a decade? But the discovery of *Feline Teleportation*, the book's disappearance and reappearance, the strange experience of visiting Mort, and even the unexpected friendship with Alder, a boy she'd thought she hated, were causing her to reexamine everything she'd thought she knew.

What other secrets did the universe hold? If cats could portal hop and enemies could become friends, what else might be possible?

Two of the chapters were each just a single page: there was "Chapter Three: Training Your Teleportation-Gifted Feline," which simply read: "You cannot train a cat to teleport. You cannot train a cat to do anything it has not independently decided to do on its own. Perhaps the book you are looking for is *Canine Psychics, a History.*"

And there was "Chapter Nine: Other Animals That Teleport," which read: "There are no other animals that teleport. But opossums and other marsupial souls can inhabit certain pockets of time."

This piece of information excited Oak so much that it set her to trembling, and she reported it in an eager whisper to Alder on the bus.

"That's why Mort is there," he said, eyes widening. "He's a marsupial."

"Yes," said Oak. "Pockets."

Pockets in space. Pockets in cats' ears. Pockets on marsupials' stomachs.

In some ways, Oak felt that her world was expanding like an accordion.

But in other ways, things felt . . . stuck. For one thing, she wished that Alder were a bit more interested in exploring the possibility of teleporting with the kittens. She'd tried to broach the subject several times, but although Alder was very interested in the *concept* of feline teleportation, he didn't seem particularly interested in the *execution* of it.

"Execution" was a poor word choice, and one that Oak would definitely avoid using around Alder. He was such a worrywart, and much more of a homebody than Oak could ever be. His sense of adventure was happily contained in trying a new brand of chocolate chips in a cookie recipe.

And Oak missed her dad more and more. Originally, the plan had been for him to move down by the end of September, but various work-related issues had delayed this, and now his move date was "up in the air."

Mom seemed oblivious to how much Oak missed her dad. Everything was working out just fine for *her*, Oak thought. She'd gotten the new job she wanted and the new house she wanted and the new upstairs bedroom she wanted. And when Oak complained one afternoon about how long it had been since she'd seen her dad, Mom just said, "Absence makes the heart grow fonder," which was the dumbest thing Oak had ever *heard*.

Rather than say something back that she might regret later, Oak just turned on her heel and went to her room, shutting the door rather loudly, with enough of a bang to wake Walnut from his slumber on her pillow. He fluffed up, his claws poked out, and he hissed.

"Sorry, Walnut," she sighed, and she shuffled in her socks across the room to pet him. But when her hand touched his fur, she felt a sudden jolt of static electricity, and both she and Walnut yelped with the shock of it.

Walnut leaped down from the bed and darted under it, retreating to a far corner.

"Oh!" said Oak, and she clambered down to the floor, lifting up the bed skirt to peer beneath. Walnut's eyes glowed, two amber orbs. "Sorry, Nutters." She touched the metal edge of the bed frame to make sure the static was gone and then reached way beneath the bed to scratch the kitten's head. After a moment, he accepted her touch, began to purr, and came out from his hiding place.

When Oak woke the next morning, her eyes were so dry that she practically had to peel them open. Walnut was asleep on her head; she scooted him gently to the side and slipped from bed, stumbling to the bathroom to splash cold water on her face. Her mouth tasted dry and sticky, so she headed to the kitchen for a glass of juice.

Her mother was standing at the kitchen window, staring outside. Leaves whirled in the grass, and several large palm fronds were strewn around the yard too, from the tree across the street. Oak got some juice and joined her mother at the window.

"Sleep okay?" Mom asked.

Oak shook her head. "I had weird dreams."

"The Santa Anas can do that," Mom said.

"The Santa Anas?"

Oak's mom gestured at the yard. "This weather," she said. "It gets like this here in the fall. Hot, dry, strong winds. Fire season, some people call it." She looked away from the window, to Oak. "You can wear shorts today if you want. It'll be hot as summer outside."

She was right; it *was* hot outside. When they left the house together—Mom to drive to the office, Oak to walk to the bus stop—Oak's hair whipped into her eyes. Her mom laughed and said, "It's days like this that make my haircut seem like an especially good idea!" She kissed Oak goodbye and got into her car. Oak watched her drive up the street before she turned to walk to the bus stop.

She stood on the corner and bent down to scratch her leg. The air was so *dry*. Her fingernails left long white marks where she'd scratched.

Here was Alder, coming up the block. His hair was a wild puff, blowing this way and that in the wind. He was walking slowly, his eyes scanning the street. It looked like he was saying something, but Oak couldn't hear him over the sound of the wind in the trees.

When he got closer, she saw that his eyes were red and puffy.

"Alder? Are you all right?"

"Fern is missing." Alder's voice cracked. "Mom had to

leave early for an appointment, and she must not have closed the door all the way. Or the wind blew it open. But Fern is gone!"

"Oh no," said Oak. She looked up and down the streets: palm fronds and dry leaves, and parked cars, and nothing more.

The bus would be there any second. They had to act fast. Oak grabbed Alder's arm. "Come on," she said.

"Where are we going? What are doing?" said Alder.

"We're going to find her," Oak said.

Alder looked over his shoulder, up toward the corner. Oak could hear the bus's familiar squeak as it pulled to a stop.

"Hurry," said Oak, and she crouched behind a parked car. Alder crouched beside her.

They stayed perfectly still and waited. At last, the bus pulled away. Then the only sounds were the wind and their own breathing.

"Okay," Oak said. "Let's go."

They dumped their backpacks in the front hall of Alder's house.

"Let's just check again, to make sure she's not sleeping in a closet or something."

"I checked everywhere," Alder said.

"Just in case," said Oak, and he nodded.

They looked in all the closets and cabinets and drawers; they even dumped out the yarn from the knitting basket. They looked behind the books on the shelves; they looked behind the curtain in the bathtub. They looked under Alder's bed, and his mother's. No Fern.

Then they went outside and scoured the yards, front and back. They peered under bushes and beneath the porch steps. "Fern!" they called. "Here, kitty! Fern!"

But even as they searched, Oak knew that Fern wasn't there. She could *feel* it. The air was dry, electric, practically crackling. Walnut sat in the front window of Oak's house and scratched at the glass like he knew what they were doing, like he wanted to help.

At last, Oak had to admit it. "Okay," she said. "She's not here."

"I told you," said Alder, and his voice was high-pitched with worry.

As much as Oak had wanted to try to teleport again, this wasn't the way she wanted it to happen. With a missing kitten and Alder on the verge of tears. From his seat in the window, Walnut yowled.

"Maybe Fern just popped away for a little bit," Oak suggested. "Maybe she'll be back soon."

"Maybe," Alder said. "But what if she's stuck, wherever she teleported to? What if there's not enough energy, like in her . . . you know . . ."

"Henry's pocket," Oak said.

"Yes!" said Alder. "Her Henry's pocket! What if there's not enough energy stored up for a return trip home?" His eyes were wide and wet. "I have a bad feeling, Oak."

Oak nodded, taking charge. "We'll get her back," she said. "There's a chapter in the book about this. . . ."

She headed for her house, and Alder followed. When she opened her front door, Walnut tried to bolt. "Oh no, you don't," Oak said, blocking his path with her foot and then bending to scoop him up. "One missing kitty is plenty." After they were inside, she closed the front door firmly behind them.

Alder went to the couch and slumped down glumly. Walnut rubbed against his leg as if to cheer him up.

It was strange to be home like this—in the middle of the morning, when she was supposed to be at school. She'd get in trouble, probably. But she'd think about that later. First, they had to find Fern.

Feline Teleportation was right where Oak had left it—tucked into her pillowcase. She grabbed it and went to join Alder on the couch. "Okay," she said. And she turned to chapter 11—"CATASTROPHE! Your Teleporting Feline Is Lost. What to Do?"

"Sometimes," the chapter began, "in spite of their best intentions and most independent attitudes, an intrepid traveler requires assistance. If you are very fortunate, and if the weather is particularly dry, and if you possess an item an auxiliary cat particularly loves, you may be able to convince that cat to lead you to the wayward traveler."

What followed was a description of how to help a cat decide to teleport ("Remember," read the book, "you can't *make* a cat do anything"). Oak skimmed through the instructions as Alder sat beside her, reading over her shoulder but obviously too worried to really take anything in.

"Do you still have that ball of yarn that Walnut likes?"

"The green one? Yes," said Alder.

"Good," said Oak. "That's his favorite. And it *is* especially dry outside. Because of the Santa Ana winds."

Oak remembered petting Walnut the night before—the way his fur had stood on end, the shock of static electricity. Today was even drier. Oak's thoughts felt as electric and wild as that spark.

She wondered. If the day was dry enough—if there was enough electricity in the air—maybe they really could help Walnut to catch it. To harness it. And, as on the day with the lightning storm, maybe they could create a strong enough current to hitch a ride with Walnut. Only this time, on purpose.

"It's perfect weather for teleporting," she said. "We'll just have to hope Walnut knows where to take us."

Alder nodded, tight-lipped and worried. "I'll go get the green yarn," he said.

"Don't forget a wool sweater!" Oak called. "And your sneakers!"

The door clicked tight behind Alder, and Oak stood to rummage for the things she would need. Walnut seemed to understand what Oak was doing; he followed her, purring, through the house.

Oak found one of her dad's wool sweaters hanging in the entry hall; she pulled it on and caught a whiff of his scent, the pine deodorant he wore, and it reminded her again of how much she missed him. "I'll think about that later," she said, half to herself, half to Walnut, and went looking for her thickest-soled shoes.

Then, dressed in rubber-soled shoes and an unseasonably warm wool sweater, kitten tucked under her arm, Oak headed for the stump of the walnut tree, where Alder waited for her, green yarn ball in hand.

"You're sure this won't hurt him?" asked Alder.

"Walnut won't be the one getting the shock," said Oak, doing her best to make her voice sound totally confident. "*We* will."

"I still don't get it," Alder said, sounding slightly panicked. Doing her best to remain calm, Oak explained again.

"On days when the air is really dry, like today," she began, "there's more electricity in the air. And so we're going to help Walnut harness it. Hopefully, when he teleports, he'll be able to take us with him."

Alder pulled at the neck of the sweater he was wearing. It was, Oak noticed, the one he'd been finishing for Beck. It was almost done, and Alder had even added a small pocket over the heart.

"I know it's too hot for a sweater," Oak said, "but wool is an excellent conductive material. Like fur."

Alder nodded. He held the green yarn ball out to Walnut. "Hey, Nutters," he said, and he sounded as if he was on the verge of tears, "if you can, help us find your sister, okay? Take us to her, wherever she is, so we can help her get home."

Walnut sniffed the yarn, and then he rubbed his face against it and began to purr.

Oak made sure her rubber-soled shoes were comfortably steady on the dry wood stump and motioned for Alder to do the same. Then she began to pet Walnut, who rested one paw on the ball of yarn. He tilted his ears forward, as if he understood what Oak was trying to do. Did the pockets of Walnut's ears spread open, just a bit, or did Oak imagine it?

Either way, Oak sensed that the time was right, and she stopped petting her kitten, extending her finger toward Alder, who reached his hand out in reply.

Just before their fingers touched, a blue spark leaped from their fingertips, arcing in a bow, connecting them, closing a circuit, and opening a door.

CHAPTER 25

"Children!" said Mort. He sounded genuinely thrilled to see them again. "You've returned!"

Alder blinked, feeling a bit off-kilter, and looked around. He was standing, just as before, in the entry hall of a house that had not existed just a moment before. He had the strange sensation of having not moved a step but, at the same time, having been transported an immeasurable distance. It took him a moment to get his bearings, but as soon as he did, he said, "Hello, Mort. Have you seen my kitten?"

"Hmm," answered the opossum, touching together the sharp-nailed fingertips of his strange little hands. "I'm afraid I haven't noticed any visitors. . . ."

Alder's heart tightened as if there were a band around it.

In Oak's arms, Walnut struggled to be released. Oak set him down, and as soon as his paws touched the floor, he ran off like an orange bolt, disappearing around the corner in the hallway.

"Walnut!" Oak called after him.

"Oh dear," said Mort, "oh my." He looked on the verge of freezing up once again, but then—

Meow.

Mew.

Here they came, sauntering back to the hallway, one orange kitten—Walnut—followed by the other—Fern!

"Oh, those sneaky kitties," Mort said, relaxing.

"Fern!" Alder half cried her name. He knelt down, and Fern pushed her forehead against his knee as if nothing strange had happened at all.

"The gang's all here," said Mort. He began to prance in place, his strange little boots clip-clopping on the wood floor. "Such a delight!" He giggled, a rather unsettling sound, especially as it emerged from those rows of yellow sharp teeth, but Alder was so relieved to be reunited with his kitten that he grinned in return.

"Hello, Mort," said Oak. "It's nice to see you again."

"I was hoping you'd come back," said Mort. "As soon as the wind picked up, I thought, well, this *is* traveling weather, and I set right to work making refreshments, just in case. I remember last visit, you said that cider upsets

241

your tummy, is that correct?"

"Ye-es," Oak said slowly.

Mort clapped his tiny hands. "Well," he said, "this time I've prepared a spot of tea. How does that sound, hmm?" He turned toward the living room.

Behind Mort's back, Alder whispered to Oak, "Can we drink his tea, do you think?"

"I don't remember anything in *Feline Teleportation* about eating or drinking in a portal world," Oak whispered back. "But I remember reading a story once where a girl ate six pomegranate seeds in the underworld, and then she had to spend half of each year there. Only that was Greek mythology, so it's probably not the same."

Still, Alder thought, better safe than sorry, so he said to Mort, "We just finished our tea, right before we came."

"Oh," said Mort, looking a bit disappointed. "Well, I hope you won't think me rude if I have a cup, just the same. It's ready to pour, you see." He gestured to a small table in front of the fire; upon it squatted a teapot gently steaming.

"Please," said Alder, "we insist."

Like a fussy old man, Mort bustled over to the side table and poured a long amber stream from the pot into one of the three teacups. "I do like to drink my tea before it's had a chance to oversteep," he explained, and his nose twitched rather adorably as he sniffed the fragrant liquid. Behind him, the fire sparked and cracked. "I'll set out cream for the kittens," he said, pouring some into a saucer and putting it on the floor in front of the fire. "They so enjoyed it last time, and travel does deplete a kitten, don't you agree?"

If they'd already had a drink of cream last time they were here, Alder couldn't see what harm could come of allowing them to have another, and so when Fern and Walnut headed toward the saucer, he didn't stop them.

Oak must have come to the same conclusion, because she didn't stop the kittens either, instead sitting in the same spot on the couch she'd sat in last time they'd visited.

Alder followed Oak's lead. Now that he knew Fern was safe, he could feel himself relaxing.

"It's such a treat, don't you think," said Mort, "to sit with a nice hot drink?"

Alder and Oak both nodded.

Mort took a rather noisy sip and then set down the teacup. His hands, though grotesque at first glance, were actually quite beautiful up close. From the cuff of Mort's sleeve came a second cuff, this one of fur, which ended neatly above his five pink fingers. Each finger was tipped with a long, curved claw that looked, Alder decided, very much like the human fingernails in the pictures from the World Nail Competition that he and Marcus had researched. Those nails, he remembered, were considered beautiful if their shape mimicked the golden ratio.

Suddenly, Alder pictured a hand strumming a banjo,

fingers flying. Two fingertips—those of the index and the middle fingers—were each capped with an upside-down golden claw.

That was what his father had called the finger picks he'd worn when he played—his golden claws. Suddenly, and completely, and for the very first time, Alder remembered his father's hands.

"Is my dad here?"

Alder hadn't known he was going to ask that question until he had blurted it out, and he found that with the question came a hot flood of tears.

"Oh," said Mort, and he looked so agitated that Alder worried he might perhaps freeze up again, like he had last time. He lifted a cookie from the plate next to the teapot and held it out to Mort, hoping it would distract him from his agitation. And perhaps it worked. Mort took the cookie, one of his odd pink fingers brushing Alder's wrist, and then he nibbled it, his teeth shaving it away bite by bite to nothing.

"Thank you," Mort said when the cookie had disappeared. He shook out a cloth napkin and pressed it to his mouth. His whiskers vibrated with intensity.

"Alder," he began, "I'm afraid your father isn't here. I live alone, you see."

"I didn't think he *lived* with you," Alder said. He took a napkin when Mort offered it and dabbed his eyes. "I just thought that maybe . . . he might *visit*, or something."

"I'm sure he would, if he could," Mort said. "I'm certain of it."

Oak reached over and took Alder's hand. Her hand was warm, and soft. She squeezed Alder's, and he squeezed back. The kittens, bellies full of cream, abandoned the saucer and jumped one and then the other atop Alder's lap, as if they knew he needed them. They purred loudly, butting their heads first against one another and then against Alder's belly, and he petted them with his one free hand, and then both hands, when Oak released him so she could pet them, too.

"There is more than one way to travel," Mort said. "Energy, you know, cannot be created or destroyed. It can be harnessed and it can be let free. But it's still there, dear children. Energy never dies."

And then Oak reached her other hand over to twine around Fern's tail, and it was when all four of the children's hands were upon the kittens that the flash occurred, brilliantly bright, so bright that it filled their noses and ears and mouths as well as their eyes, and then they were home, back upon the tree stump, and Alder felt as full of wonder as ever a person could be.

CHAPTER 26

It had worked.

Amazingly, miraculously, it had worked. There was Fern, safe in Alder's arms, and here was Walnut, curled contentedly (and perhaps sleepily) in Oak's. The four of them pressed close together on the tree stump in the yard. Around them, the wind was softer now, gentle.

Oak stepped down from the stump. Alder did too.

What could someone even say in the face of such a thing? It was too big, too beautiful for words, so, with a little wave, Oak turned toward her house, and Alder did the same.

When she was safe inside, Oak found that she felt a little bit weepy and very, very tired. She kicked off her shoes and went with Walnut to her bedroom, curling up and pulling the covers over them both.

Opossums and teacups and kittens and doors. Fathers and sweaters and yarn balls and more. Howling winds. Sparkling air. Tree stumps and found books. A house that wasn't there.

Maybe she was dreaming. Maybe part of her was still traveling—some part that took longer than the body to get from one space to another, trailing behind her like a scarf. Maybe it was that part that felt confused, mixed up, and a little bit lost.

She would lie very still, Oak decided, so that the part of her that was still traveling would know where to find the rest of her. Walnut's purr grew louder, his whole being a warm, fuzzy comfort in her arms.

And then Oak was definitely asleep.

"Oak?"

Mom's voice jolted Oak awake. She sat straight up in bed, and Walnut, displeased with the sudden movement, shot out of her arms and ran from the room.

"Honey, what are you doing home?" Mom crossed the room and sat next to Oak on the bed. She felt Oak's forehead. "Are you sick?"

Mom's hand felt so good on Oak's skin. Cool, and comforting.

"The school called me at the office to say you were absent. You had me so worried!"

Oak's eyes overfilled and tears spilled down her cheeks.

And then she was sobbing, crying loud like a little kid, messy crying, and Mom put her arm around Oak's shoulders to pull her close.

At first Oak resisted, pulling away, but when Mom's arms loosened, like she was going to let Oak go, Oak collapsed instead into her mother's embrace.

Mom caught her, strong and solid, and held Oak as she cried.

"It's okay," Mom said. "It's all right."

Oak cried until her tears were gone, and then she sniffed and hiccuped and wiped her nose with her sleeve. It was rough and itchy—she was still wearing Dad's wool sweater.

Her mom pulled a tissue from the box on the nightstand and gave it to Oak. "Honey," she said again, "what are you doing home?"

"I didn't get on the bus," Oak said. "I just . . . stayed home today."

Her mom nodded. "I can see that." Her gaze traveled over the sweater Oak was wearing. "You're missing your dad," she said.

It was true. Oak nodded, sniffing.

"He'll be here soon," Mom said.

"And," Oak said, "I'm mad at you."

"Ah," said Mom. She smoothed Oak's hair from her face.

"You didn't ask me if I wanted to move. You never ask me *anything*."

Mom nodded. Even as Oak said it, she knew it wasn't completely true, though it *felt* true.

"Let me ask you something now," Mom said. "Are you sorry we moved?"

Was she sorry? No. She wasn't. Not really. "That's not the point," Oak said.

Mom laughed, but not *at* Oak. "I know," she said. Then she said, "It's okay to be mad at me, baby. You can be as mad as you need to be. I'll love you just the same."

This, Oak knew, was completely true.

Mom patted Oak's knee through the blanket. Then she looked around and said, "You know, you're right about this room. It could use some color."

"I was thinking lavender," Oak said.

"Lavender," Mom mused. "That sounds lovely. Well, what do you say?"

"You mean . . . today? Like, *now*?"

"Well, you're home from school, and I'm home from work. Why not?"

"Okay," Oak said. "But I'm still going to be mad at you." Except, right now, she wasn't.

Mom laughed. "Tough but fair," she said. She stood up. "Come on. Let's go buy some paint."

CHAPTER 27

When Alder gave Beck his finished sweater the next day in class, it was with the knowledge that the sweater had traveled to a different dimension. He liked the thought that knit into the sweater was that secret experience.

"Thanks, man," Beck said when Alder handed it to him. Alder had folded it and tied it around with a ribbon that he'd found in a box in his dining room that contained a bunch of random wrapping stuff, like scissors and tape and gift tags.

He watched as Beck set the sweater on his desk, pulled the ribbon loose, and unfolded it. The blue yarn Alder had had at home was a near-perfect match to the yarn Beck's grandmother had used. He was a little nervous about how Beck might respond to the orange pocket he'd knit and attached just above where Beck's heart would be, but Beck grinned when he saw it.

"Orange was my grammy's favorite color," he said. "How'd you know?"

Alder shrugged. He hadn't known, of course, but when he'd seen a small ball of orange yarn tucked into the bottom of the yarn basket at home, his hand had reached for it without his even thinking.

Energy can't be created or destroyed, Mort had said. Maybe it was Beck's grandmother's energy that had pulled his hand toward the orange yarn.

Probably not. But maybe.

"Thanks, man," Beck said again, and he shrugged out of his hoodie, right then and there, and pulled the sweater over his head. For a minute Alder worried that the neck hole might be too tight, but it turned out to be just fine.

"You're welcome," Alder said, and he turned to go back to his desk.

"Hey," Beck called after him. "Want to sit with me and Marcus today at lunch?"

Slowly, Alder turned around. A month ago, he wouldn't have hesitated. Heck, if he was being honest, this was exactly the sort of invitation he'd been daydreaming about. But now . . .

"I've got a better idea," Alder said.

✳ ✴ ✳

It was a tight fit, but they all managed to squeeze around the lunch table—Beck and Marcus, Oak and Alder, Miriam and Cynthia and the twins.

At first, it was awkward, and Alder worried he'd made a mistake, inviting Beck and Marcus to join him and the girls. Beck and Marcus sat side by side at the end of one bench, with Alder next to Marcus and Oak on his left; across from them sat the other kids. Alder couldn't help but feel like he was the hinge connecting the pair of boys to his right to the rest of the table. It was a big responsibility, being a hinge.

But then Oak caught his eye, and she must have been able to see how uncomfortable he felt, because suddenly she pushed the contents of her lunch—two sliced-up oranges, a sandwich cut into quarters, a bag of potato chips, and three homemade oatmeal chocolate chip cookies—into the center of the table. "Let's have a potluck," she said, as if this were a thing they did all the time.

There was a moment of silence, and Alder wasn't sure what anyone else thought of the idea. But then Beck said, "Cool!" and he pushed his lunch into the center too—a couple of slices of cold pizza, a peach, and a whole sleeve of Thin Mint cookies.

It was the sleeve of Thin Mints that started the cascade. Everyone wanted in on those, and soon Miriam and Cynthia had added their sandwiches to the mix (gluten-free turkey and peanut butter and jelly), along with Carmen and Cameron's veggie slices and ranch dressing, tortilla chips and guacamole. Marcus was the last to push in his food, but he did it, and with a grin.

"You're still eating egg salad every day?" Alder asked.

"It's the best sandwich," Marcus said with a shrug.

And just like that, things were okay between them.

They laughed and talked and shared the lot of it.

It was a disgusting mix of turkey and egg, of ranch dressing and Thin Mints.

It was the best lunch Alder had ever had.

He and Oak rode the bus home at the end of the day in happy silence. The world, Alder felt, seemed to make sense in a way it hadn't since the school year began.

What Mr. Rivera had said was true, he decided. Everything *was* connected—language arts and math, kittens and portals, old friends and new friends, past and present. It was also true that things were complicated in ways Alder hadn't known them to be, and it was true he didn't understand all of it. But that was okay, he thought, settling comfortably back into the vinyl bus bench as they bounced along toward home. He didn't need to know everything.

The world was full of twists and turns and magic and surprises, and that was okay. It was good.

"See ya, tree kids," Faith called as Alder followed Oak down the steps.

"See ya, Faith," they answered in unison.

Together, Oak and Alder walked down Rollingwood Drive. Neither of their mothers' cars were in the driveways.

"Want to come over?" Alder asked.

"Sure," said Oak. "I'll grab Walnut and we'll be over soon."

Alder opened his front door and found the mail had arrived, pushed through the slot. He picked it up and set it in the basket next to the door, where mail was always set.

He heard the thump of Fern jumping down from her little bed in the front window, followed by her meow that he knew was her way of saying hello.

"Hey there, kitty," he called, turning to pick her up, but before he did, the top letter caught his eye—it was addressed to him, Alder Madigan.

And the sender was Family Tree.

"Oh," said Alder, pleased. "The DNA results arrived!"

Fern purred and wound between Alder's feet, her orange fluffy tail wrapping around his calf. He'd get a snack, Alder decided, bending down to scratch Fern's head, and then he'd open the letter. Maybe Oak had gotten her results too, and they could compare. That would be fun, he thought to himself as he kicked off his shoes and turned toward the kitchen.

It was at that moment, behind him, that his front door

banged open so hard that it hit the wall. Fern yowled and dashed down the hallway, disappearing into Alder's room. Oak filled the doorway, her energy electric, her hair a mess around her head. She wore, Alder noticed, a single shoe. And in one hand she clutched an envelope identical to Alder's, except hers was torn open.

Her other hand clutched the test results.

"Alder," she said, and the sound of her voice made all the hairs on his body stand on end. "We're cousins."

CHAPTER 28

It was impossible. But it was true.

The test didn't lie—*science* didn't lie. At the end of her results, in a section with the heading "Relatives," it read:

> *Alder Madigan*
> *Possible Range: 1st Cousin*
> *Confidence: Extremely High*
> *Shared DNA: 897 cM across 33 segments*

Oak had no idea what "897 cM across 33 segments" meant, but she knew what "Extremely High" confidence meant.

And she knew what "1st Cousin" meant.

Facts were facts, and science was science.

She watched as Alder scanned her test results, his face wrinkling up in the way it did when he was confused.

"This doesn't make any sense," he said.

"Let's open yours," Oak suggested, "to make sure."

Alder nodded. He handed Oak back her test results, and then he tried to open his envelope, but his fingers were shaking.

"Let me do it," Oak said, and Alder handed the envelope over to her. They were still standing in the entry hall, and, Oak decided, Alder looked like he needed to sit down. So she led the way to his couch, and Alder followed.

When they were sitting, Oak tore open Alder's envelope with a sharp rip. Out came his test results, folded neatly in thirds. She hesitated, then handed the paper to Alder. They were *his*, after all; he should see them first. He turned to the end, to the page that listed his relationships with other users of the service. Oak was sitting close enough that she could read the sheet too, and even though a moment ago she'd magnanimously thought that Alder should get to see his results before she did, it was impossible not to peek.

They gasped together:

Oak Carson
Possible Range: 1st Cousin
Confidence: Extremely High
Shared DNA: 897 cM across 33 segments

"That's you," Alder whispered.

Oak nodded. It was.

"How is this possible?" Alder asked. "What does it mean?"

"It means," said Oak, "that somehow, one of your parents is the brother or sister of either my mom or my dad. It means we're family."

Alder lowered his results to his lap. He looked up at Oak, and the expression on his face made tears spring to her eyes, though she wasn't sure what it meant.

"Family," he said. "I've . . . never had much family before."

Oak laughed, and it was strange how her throat felt so thick. "Me either," she said.

"Cousins," Alder said, like he was trying out the word.

"Cousins," Oak answered.

Alder grinned. "And imagine," he said, "how much we hated each other at first!"

Oak laughed. "Families fight sometimes, I guess."

Alder laughed too, and he tilted back his head just the way Oak knew *she* did when she laughed . . . just the way her mother did as well.

How had she never noticed it before? Was it because she hadn't known to look? Alder's hair—it was dark and curly, the way Oak's mother's had been, before she'd started to wear it shorn so close to her head. And hadn't Oak's mom told her that she used to live here, in LA, that she'd grown up here even?

"Alder," said Oak, "I think my mom is your aunt."

"Really?" said Alder, blinking. "Are you sure?"

Oak nodded. "Pretty sure," she said. "But there's only one way to be certain."

Alder immediately knew what she was suggesting. "We can't ask her," he said, horrified. "If she wanted us to know, she would have told us."

"My mom isn't big on telling me things," Oak said. "She didn't even tell me that we were moving down here until the day she started bringing home boxes to pack."

"Do you think . . . ," Alder began, "that your mom is related to my mom, or to my dad?"

Oak shrugged. "I've only met your mom that one time. What do *you* think? Do I look more like your mom or dad?" She squared her shoulders and tried to make her face as blank as possible so that Alder could imagine his parents onto it.

He looked at her for a long time. It was sort of uncomfortable, honestly, to be looked at like that. She saw his eyes look into hers, and then up across her forehead, and over her hair, and at her nose and mouth and chin, and the whole thing was disconcerting.

Finally, "Can you sing?" Alder asked.

"Nope," Oak answered.

At this, Alder sighed a little, as if he was disappointed. And Oak maybe understood why; if she were Canary's niece, then Alder would have another connection to his dad in the world.

"It's got to be my mom," Alder said at last. "Maybe you guys have the same nose? I don't think you look like my dad."

Oak nodded. That's what she'd thought, too, though she didn't want to be the first one to say it. "Either way," she said, "it means we're cousins."

Alder nodded. "Cousins," he echoed. "Wow."

They sat on the couch together. Together, they thought about family. It was a while before either of them spoke.

"I wonder what happened that made our moms not talk to each other anymore," Alder said at last.

"Well," said Oak, "my mom can have a pretty bad temper. Sometimes she says things she doesn't mean."

"My mom tends to be kind of a hermit," Alder admitted. "She mostly likes to hang out with me and be at home, unless she's volunteering or working at the co-op. She's not good about having friends and stuff like that. I don't even remember the last time she went out to dinner with someone other than me."

"*My* mom is kind of a workaholic," Oak said. "When she's not at her work office, she's in the bedroom that she made into a home office. She's not really great with friends either. She says there are things she misses about San Francisco, but I don't even know if that's true."

"Wow," said Alder. "Wow."

"We have to ask them," Oak said. "We have to know."

Alder chewed on his lip. But then he said, "Okay. We'll ask them tonight."

The best time to ask a hard question, they decided, was over a good meal. And so they set to work.

Oak went home to get four potatoes and butter and cheese (and Walnut, and her other shoe); then she set the potatoes to baking while Alder heated up water to make boxes of macaroni and cheese. While the water was boiling and the potatoes were in the oven, they worked together to make a salad. The kittens sat side by side on Alder's kitchen table and watched, their eyes flicking back and forth as Alder and Oak moved about the kitchen.

"Did you leave a note for your mom?" Alder asked.

"Uh-huh," said Oak. "Right on the fridge, where she couldn't miss it." She grinned. "I wrote that the neighbors invited us over for dinner."

"Well, if you count me and Fern as 'the neighbors' and leave my mom out if it," Alder said, laughing, "then it's true!"

The kitchen was warm with cooking and music—Alder had set one of Canary's records to spinning—by the time Alder's mom pushed through the door just after six o'clock.

"Alder," she called, "are you cooking?"

Oak heard the clickety-clack of Alder's mom's clogs as she crossed the living room and entered the kitchen. She wore a big bright smile; a lavender scarf looped around her neck, clashing prettily with her light-red hair, which fell in waves across her shoulders.

My aunt, Oak found herself thinking, and her face split into a big dumb grin.

"Oh," Alder's mother said, faltering, when she saw Oak standing in her kitchen. "Alder, I didn't know you had a friend over."

"Hi, Mom," Alder said. "Remember our neighbor, Oak? She and her mom are coming over for dinner."

Oak noticed that Alder had made it a statement rather than a question.

"O-oh," said Alder's mom. "Hello."

"Hi," said Oak. She stuck out her hand to shake and then noticed that some of the cheese she'd been grating for the potatoes was stuck to her fingertips. She wiped her hand on her jeans and then stuck it out again.

Alder's mom shook it, and her face softened into a smile. "I should have invited you over sooner. I'm glad my son is more . . . neighborly than I've been."

"Oh, that's okay," said Oak.

"No, it's not," Greta said. "I really should have introduced myself to you and your parents—your mother?—sooner."

"My dad is moving down pretty soon," Oak explained. "He had to stay back in San Francisco for work, so Mom and I moved first, because of her job and so I could start school with everyone else."

"Oh, I see," Greta said, and then, "Alder, can I help with anything?"

There was a knock at the door. "I'll get it," Oak said. "It'll be my mom."

And it was—still wearing her suit and heels from the office. She hadn't even stopped to take off her earrings. "Oak," she said. "What's going on? You left me a note?"

Oak opened the door more widely, as if this was her home. There was, she noticed, a patch of lavender paint on Mom's wrist, left over from yesterday's project. It was exactly the shade of Alder's mom's scarf. Maybe it was a sign. Maybe it meant something. "Mom," she said. "Hi."

Behind her was the sound of Greta's clogs, and then there was Greta. "Hello," she said to Oak's mom. "Won't you please come in?"

Oak's mom hesitated, and for a brief moment Oak was filled with sick dread at the thought that she might rudely refuse. But then her mom put on her work voice—the tone she used when someone from the architecture firm called—and she said, "Thank you so much for the invitation. I'm Olivia. It's lovely to meet you." She crossed the threshold and held out her hand to shake.

Oak felt as if the room was spinning. This wasn't the

way it was supposed to go—they were supposed to recognize each other. She looked toward the kitchen to find Alder in the doorway, looking as confused as Oak felt.

"I'm Greta," said Alder's mom, and she gestured to the kitchen. "It seems our kids made us a meal. Shall we?"

And Oak and her mother followed Greta through to the next room, where Oak's mom introduced herself to Alder, and the four of them filled their plates. As they did, the moms asked each other polite questions about what they did for work.

"I . . . I don't think they've ever met," Alder whispered to Oak as he speared a cheese-covered baked potato half.

"Clearly," Oak whispered back, piercing the other half and plopping it on her plate.

The four of them went into the dining room, where Canary's croon filled the space, and the cats meowed and purred and wound in and out of the table legs.

They all sat down, and Oak's mom and Greta laughed about what a coincidence it was that they'd adopted sibling kittens. This, Oak decided, was as good a segue as they were going to find.

"Mom," she blurted, "do *you* have any siblings?"

"Don't be silly, Oak, you know I'm an only child."

"Me too," said Greta. "I'd always hoped for a brother, but no luck."

"To only children," Oak's mom said, raising her water glass.

264

"To only children," Greta echoed, raising hers, and Alder and Oak had no real choice but to follow suit.

"To only children," they muttered, and the four glasses tinkled as they all brought them to the center of the table and clinked them in a toast.

CHAPTER 29

It was a perfectly nice dinner. Oak's mother even apologized to Alder's mom for cutting down the big tree without talking about it first.

"I can get a bit overzealous with my plans," she said. "I don't always think about how the things I do might affect other people."

Alder noticed that Oak nodded a little when her mom said this, and he knew that she was thinking about their move to Southern California, and everything that had meant to Oak.

Alder's mom apologized to Oak's mom for not being neighborly. "I should have brought you cookies or offered to help you get to know the neighborhood," she admitted, "but honestly, I was just so angry about the tree. And sad.

It was like a member of the family." She nodded to the portrait hanging on the wall.

All four of them turned to look.

"That's my dad," Alder explained. "He died when I was little."

"Oh," said Oak's mom. Her eyes widened as if now she understood better about the tree. She turned away from the portrait, back toward Alder and his mom. When she spoke again, her voice was quietly serious. "I was wrong to cut down that tree without speaking with you first," she said. "And the other day, when Oak said something about me cutting it down—well, it hit me then how awful it was of me to make such a decision all on my own. Just because the tree grew on our property didn't mean that it really belonged just to us. I was only thinking of myself. I hope you can forgive me. Both of you."

The apology wouldn't bring the tree back, of course. The past can't be changed. But Alder was glad when his mom reached over to hug Oak's mom, when she said that she was forgiven. It made Alder feel proud, the way she did that. And then the two moms agreed to have a fresh start, and by the end of the meal the two of them were laughing together about the big pothole up on Silver Spur Road, wondering what it would take to get it filled.

"Oak and I will do the dishes," Alder offered when everyone had finished eating.

"Yeah," Oak agreed, jumping up. They began gathering the plates and silverware.

"Well, thank you, Alder," said his mom.

Of course, Alder wasn't only being polite. He wanted to talk to Oak, away from their mothers' ears. "I don't understand," he said, his voice low, as they stacked dishes in the sink.

"Maybe there's something wrong with the test results," said Oak.

Alder filled the sink with warm water and squirted in dish soap to make bubbles. "Maybe," he said. He didn't want that to be true. He wanted Oak to be his cousin. He wanted family.

In the dining room, he heard his mom get up and flip the record to the other side. It was one of Canary's albums; When Alder had put it on earlier, he hadn't been thinking about everyone listening to it. But it didn't bother him, the way it once would have, to have the music playing. Instead, it felt comforting, as he dipped his hands into the warm, bubbly water, to hear his father's crooning voice floating through the house. "We'll figure it out," he said to Oak, and hope rose in him like a bubble.

She nodded. "You wash, I'll rinse," she said, and then they fell into a rhythm—Alder rubbing each soapy dish with a sponge, then passing it to Oak, who ran it under fresh water and set it in the drying rack on the counter.

Suddenly, the kittens, who had been curled into one of the yarn baskets in the corner of the dining room, both leaped up and began meowing. They trotted into the kitchen and wound in and out of Oak's and Alder's legs, rubbing their heads against them, their meows becoming more like yowls.

"What is it, kitties?" Oak asked. "What got you so excited?"

Their tails, Alder noticed, were puffed up, as if by electricity.

And then the doorbell rang.

Oak and Alder froze, dishes in hands, cats between feet.

"It couldn't be Mort," Oak hissed. Somehow, that was the exact thing Alder had been thinking.

Maybe it *was* Mort, though, Alder thought. After all, stranger things—or equally strange things—had happened.

He grabbed a dish towel and dried his hands on the way to the door. His hand reached for the doorknob and hesitated, hovering, for a long moment before he grabbed it, turned it, and opened the door.

Mort was not standing on the other side.

But a man was, one who looked oddly familiar.

"Hello," said the man, smiling. "I'm looking for my family."

✳ ✦ ✳

His family. Alder opened his mouth, but nothing came out. The man wore a lustrous beard, red tinged. His hair, dark blond, thinning, was brushed back from his brow. There were long wavy wrinkles across his forehead and branches of smaller wrinkles in the corner of each of his brown eyes, which were framed by square brown glasses. He was tall and thin, much taller than Alder. He wore a green T-shirt that was torn slightly at the neck and stretched out as if it was an old shirt, a favorite. He had on light blue jeans with paint spatters on the thighs; one of the knees looked about worn through. On his feet were orange sneakers.

As if by way of explanation, he held out a piece of paper he'd been holding. "My family is here?" he asked.

Alder recognized Oak's handwriting—the note she'd left her mom. Tears filled his eyes, and as he blinked, they spilled over, wetting his cheeks, catching in his eyelashes and making the whole world sparkle.

"Yes," Alder said, and he opened the door wide. "Your family is here. Please come in."

Oak's father stepped across the threshold. Oak was still in the kitchen, and the moms were still in the dining room. The kittens trotted over to the man and purred as they rubbed against his legs. He laughed, squatting down to pet them.

"Well, hello there," he said, and just then the song that

was playing—Canary's song—rose into a crescendo, his warm, rich voice filling the whole house, as if someone had suddenly turned up the volume:

Wandering down the railroad tracks away from my sweet
   home
Wondering on the railroad tracks where I next will roam
Whispering on the railroad tracks why the wind has blown
Wandering down the railroad tracks away from my sweet
   home

Kneeling, Oak's father froze, one hand holding the note, the other on a kitten's head. His head was tilted up, his eyes blind, as if he searched for a face he could not see.

No one moved—not Alder, not the man, not the cats. Not on the outside. But as Canary's voice wailed and cried out about home, about leaving home, Alder felt his insides shifting. As if they were making room for something, as if a pocket he hadn't known was there was pulled wide open.

"Is that—" Oak's dad began.

"It's Canary Madigan," Alder said. "Your brother."

Time, Alder learned, really can stop.

The man who was his uncle knelt, and Alder stood, and to their right, on the bookshelf, Mort silently watched. The air fell still. The kittens made no sound. And Canary held one note, the last note—"*home.*"

It could have been a second. It could have been a minute. It could have been forever. But it wasn't forever, because the last note ended, and the kittens purred, and the man stood.

"Are you . . ."

"Your nephew," Alder said. And he nodded.

There were footsteps coming from the kitchen.

"Alder," said Oak, "what are you—" She broke off suddenly, and Alder turned to see her expression. It was shock, first, when she saw who had come to the door; it froze her in place for a long moment as her brain made sense of seeing her father right there in front of her, when Alder knew she hadn't expected him to arrive anytime soon.

And then, joy. A wide happy grin, a chirp of glee, as she rushed across the room and threw herself into his arms, which opened to catch her.

"Dad," she said, and then her words were muffled into her father's shirt, and he laughed and lifted her up off the floor.

"I decided to surprise you," he said, and his voice was rough with emotion.

"You grew a beard," Oak said.

"I sure did," he said.

More footsteps—the moms this time.

"Carter?" said Oak's mom as she rounded the corner, and then again when she saw him, "*Carter.*"

Then it was the three of them hugging—Oak and her dad and her mom, Oak squished between her parents, and Alder felt a flash of something—of yearning—as he watched, but then his mom came over and pulled him close into her side.

The cats purred so loudly it seemed there was a motor running somewhere; they purred and they rubbed everybody's legs and they circled around until one of them nipped the other's neck playfully, and then they pounced and rolled and kicked their hind legs like bunnies.

At last, Oak and her mom and her dad broke apart, and she turned to Alder and said, "Alder, I want to introduce you to my dad."

"Your name is Alder?" her dad said. "Like the tree?"

Alder nodded. Words, it seemed, had escaped him.

Oak's dad shook his head, but not like he didn't believe it. Rather, like he *did* believe it. "We said we'd name our kids after trees," he said softly. "It's one promise we both kept, I guess."

"Dad?" said Oak.

He turned to her. "Honey, I'd like to introduce *you* to someone. My nephew, Alder."

CHAPTER 30

"**I** should have told you about my brother," Oak's dad said. "But the truth is, I was ashamed."

They were sitting—all of them, Oak and her parents and Alder and his mom and the kittens—in Alder's front room. Oak's dad and mom were side by side on the pink velvet couch, holding hands. Alder's mom sat in the tall blue chair.

Oak sat with Alder on the floor across from the couch. She let her shoulder press into Alder's shoulder so he would know she was right there. He was trembling a little.

Her dad said, "Let me tell you about him now." He blinked, staring off as if looking back in time. Then he said, his words rushing like water undammed, "My brother and I were like two strings on a banjo. Close as could be, and meant to be played together. He was my little brother. I was four years older. He was born with the same dark, wavy hair he had all his life. He was a chubby, milky baby with a smile for everyone. When he was little, he'd follow me everywhere I went, and he made the cutest chirping sound. That's why we called him Canary at first. Later we kept calling him that because of the way he could sing."

From where she sat next to Alder, Oak could see the portrait that hung on the wall of the dining room. Baby Alder and his mom and his dad. Her *uncle*, who she would never get to meet. She pressed her arm into Alder's again. He was warm, and solid, and right there.

Her dad continued. "Our band, the one we planned to start one day—we called it Canary and the Coal Miners. I'd be one of the Coal Miners, on guitar, and we'd find someone to play bass, someone else to play drums, and Canary would sing and strum the banjo. That was the plan when we were kids. But then, you know how it can be, life . . . interfered. By the time I was in high school, those four years between us might as well have stretched to forty. I know Canary was disappointed in me. Angry too. I was busy with other things, and I didn't make time for us to make music together."

Walnut hopped up onto Oak's dad's lap. He looked right at home.

"And then I went off to college," he continued. "There'd

be time later, I figured, for us to make our music. Canary was still just a kid. But soon, Canary wasn't a kid anymore. And he never quit playing, even when I did. He called me once, when he was just about to graduate high school. He wanted me to join him on the road. He wanted to give Canary and the Coal Miners a shot, he said. A real shot."

Oak's dad scratched Walnut's head.

"But I'd just finished college, and I was trying to find a job so I could start paying back those student loans. Our parents died that year, just a few months apart, and I felt this pressure to be a real grown-up. I couldn't just take off and travel around like some dumb kid, I told him. I had responsibilities. I had a *future*."

Oak's dad made a sound—a sort of laugh, a sort of choke, like he was holding back tears. Her mom laid a hand on his leg. Then he went on. "Canary didn't say much to that, though I could tell I'd hurt his feelings. He hung up, and that was that. The thing about time is that it passes. And time passed. I don't think we ever meant to stop speaking—not then. It was just that I was so busy, and then *he* was so busy. He made an album—no Coal Miners, just Canary. He'd changed his last name, too, to Madigan, and that felt to me like a real cut, like he'd severed himself from me.

"The first time I heard one of his songs on the radio, I was on my way to pick you up for a date, Olivia. And then there was his voice in my car—so clear, so beautiful . . . well, I'm ashamed to tell you that it didn't make me feel proud to hear my brother's voice. It made me feel jealous."

Oak's dad shook his head. He stopped petting Walnut. Oak watched her mom lace her fingers through her father's. He cleared his throat, like something had gotten stuck, and then continued.

"Little things can become big things, if you let them," her dad said. "I let that little thing—my jealousy—become a big thing—a reason not to stay in touch. I had my life, and Canary had his. I heard he got married around the same time I did, but we didn't go to one another's weddings. After you were born, Oak, I did send a birth announcement to the last address I had for him. But it came back marked Return to Sender."

"We had moved by then," Alder's mom said. "To this house. I suppose we never filled out a change of address form."

"I meant to track him down, but time just goes so fast. And then," Oak's dad said, and his voice grew thick, "then, the next I heard, Canary had—he had run out of time."

Next to her, Alder slumped a little, and Oak put her arm around him and rested her head on his shoulder. "I'm so sorry your dad died, Alder," she said.

Alder sniffed, wiped his cheeks. "Thanks," he said, tilting his head to rest atop Oak's.

"But now," said Alder's mom, "now, somehow, you've moved right next door."

"Right next door," Oak's dad said, his voice full of wonder. "Amazing." And then he looked at Alder. "And even more amazing—I have a nephew."

Oak heard Alder gulp nervously. He sat up straight and nodded.

"And I have a cousin," Oak said. She looked around at her parents, at Alder and his mom. She listened to Canary's voice—her uncle's voice—as it wailed and sang. Maybe Canary wasn't here with them . . . but maybe he wasn't really gone, either. After all, like Mort said, energy never dies.

"Alder," her dad said, and he got up from the couch, came around to the other side of the coffee table, and knelt down right beside them. He put his hand on Alder's shoulder, and Alder's hand reached up to meet it.

"Yes," Alder said.

They had, Oak saw, the same hands. The same long fingers. The same straight nails.

Oak's dad—Alder's uncle—spoke. "I wasn't the brother I wish I had been. I can't change that now. But I have so much to tell you about your dad. So much to share. And more than that. I promise—if you'll let me—"

"Yes," Alder said again. "Yes."

Mort here, with a riddle for you:

You can see it in the way someone looks at you.
You can hear it in the way someone sings to you.
You can taste it in the way someone cooks for you.
You can smell it in the flowers someone picks for you.
You can feel it in the way someone holds you close.

Can you guess what it is?
Alder and Oak and their grown-ups decided to build a third place, a shared space, between their houses. It wasn't big, just the size of a small room. Oak's mom drew up the blueprints, and they all pitched in to build it together, right where the old walnut tree used to be.

Inside, there was a small table with two chairs, a few games, some albums, a tea set, and a row of books on a built-in bookshelf. That's where I took up residence, right beside the record player.

They built three entrances; two of them were cat-size tunnels, one leading from Oak's house, the other from Alder's. Through these tunnels, the cats could come and go as they pleased—because siblings shouldn't be separated.

The third entrance was an unpainted wooden door. Next to the door hung two brass numbers—a 1 and a 3.

It's a strange thing, love. It's magic. It's a house you can't see, a third place between two people. It's enormous, but it can also fit inside the smallest pocket. Once you build it, love is there, even if you turn your back on it, even if you walk away.

It's waiting for you to come home.

ACKNOWLEDGMENTS

Sometimes, a story comes along that seems to know what it wants to become. *The House That Wasn't There* was such a story . . . eventually. The first time I tried to write it, years ago, it came out all wrong, an entire book different from the one you read.

Thanks to the good advice of my friend and agent Rubin Pfeffer, that version is not the book you are holding. Rubin, thank you for that advice, amid so much good advice over the years.

In its second incarnation, *The House That Wasn't There* entered the world much more smoothly. This time, it was surrounded by so many enthusiastic and supportive people. I'm especially indebted to my friend Martha Brockenbrough, who worked alongside me, whose energy and enthusiasm always buoys me; and my early readers, including my sisters Sasha and Mischa Kuczynski and my friends Nina LaCour, Laura Ruby, and Eliot Schrefer. The book is stronger because of the careful attention of each of you.

The Walden Pond team is the perfect home for this book and, I hope, many, many more. I'm indebted to my editor, Jordan Brown, whose support and care meant that I was never rushed and that the important nuances of feline teleportation were always taken seriously. Debbie Kovacs, Donna Bray, Tiara Kittrell, Molly Fehr, Amy Ryan, Vaishali Nayak, Audrey Diestelkamp, Sam Benson, and Renée Cafiero all played invaluable roles in the development of the aspects of book-making that are beyond my ken, and I am deeply grateful to you all.

Jessica Tickle, the artist who created the book's cover, made magic by illustrating the house that wasn't there in glorious negative space. Thank you so!

And my own little family—Keith, Max, and Davis—as ever, you are the doorways and the keys; you are the house where I know I am always home.